J ROBERTS
Roberts, Willo Davis.
Secrets at Hidden Valley /
33277001619357

CAMAS PUBLIC LIBRARY
CAMAS, WA

3 3277 00161 9357

New Book Shelf
Keep Until 10/98

D0458508

secrets At hidden valley

BOOKS BY WILLO DAVIS ROBERTS

The View from the Cherry Tree

Don't Hurt Laurie!

The Minden Curse

More Minden Curses

The Girl with the Silver Eyes

The Pet-sitting Peril

Baby-sitting Is a Dangerous Job

No Monsters in the Closet

Eddie and the Fairy Godpuppy

The Magic Book

Sugar Isn't Everything

Megan's Island

What Could Go Wrong?

Nightmare

To Grandmother's House We Go

Scared Stiff

Jo and the Bandit

What Are We Going to Do about David?

Caught!

*The Absolutely True Story . . . How I Visited Yellowstone
Park with the Terrible Rupes*

Twisted Summer

Secrets at Hidden Valley

WILLO DAVIS ROBERTS

SECRETS AT HIDDEN VALLEY

A JEAN KARL BOOK

ATHENEUM BOOKS FOR YOUNG READERS

CAMAS PUBLIC LIBRARY

Atheneum Books for Young Readers
An imprint of Simon & Schuster Children's Publishing Division
1230 Avenue of the Americas
New York, New York 10020

Text copyright © 1997 by Willo Davis Roberts
All rights reserved including the right of
reproduction in whole or in part in any form.

Book design by Angela Carlino
The text of this book is set in Mrs. Eaves.

First Edition
Printed in the United States of America
10 9 8 7 6 5 4 3 2 1

Library of Congress Cataloging-in-Publication Data
Roberts, Willo Davis.
Secrets at Hidden Valley / by Willo Davis Roberts.—1st ed.
p. cm.
"A Jean Karl book."
Summary: After the death of her father, Steffi lives with her disagreeable
grandfather in a recreational vehicle park where everyone seems to have a secret.
ISBN 0-689-81166-7
[1. Death—Fiction. 2. Grandfathers—Fiction.
3. Recreational vehicles—Fiction.] I. Title.
PZ7.R54465Se 1997
[Fic]—dc20
96-17576

To my granddaughter Krista

secrets At hidden Valley

1

"Honestly, Steffi," Mom said in an ominous tone as she folded a blouse carelessly and put it in the suitcase, "sometimes I wonder how I've put up with such a mouthy kid all these years."

Steffi stared at the garments going into the battered blue case. "How come I'm only mouthy when I disagree with you?"

"I haven't figured that out yet. It's settled, Steff. I'm going on location to try to earn some money for us. I told your dad he needed more life insurance, but he thought he was going to live forever, and already we've gone deeply into what we got just paying off his hospital bills. And you" —here she paused to look directly at her daughter— "are going to your grandfather's for a few months."

"I don't know my grandfather," Steffi reminded her. "*You* don't even know him, really. You only met him a few times, didn't you?"

"Twice," Audri Thomas said crisply, tucking a pair of shoes in beside the blouses and closing the lid. "Here, sit on this and help me get it latched."

Steffi obeyed, but she still felt rebellious. "You didn't like him."

"I was prepared to like him," Mom said. "*He* didn't like *me*. From what your father said, his mother and I would have gotten along, if she'd lived, but I was not what *he* wanted in a daughter-in-law."

"So what makes you think he'll like *me*? Or that I'll like *him*? Dad couldn't stand him, and Grandpa was his own father."

"Whatever caused the rift between them has nothing to do with you. He didn't tell me not to send you, so you're going. He'd have said so if he didn't want you."

Steffi bounced on the suitcase until her mother secured the latches, then took a different tack. "Why can't I just stay here with Meggie?"

"She's no relation to us, for Pete's sake. Why should she take you on?" Audri placed another bag on the bed and opened it wide. "She's too old to want the responsibility of an eleven-year-old. Besides, she hasn't asked you to stay. And I'd have to pay her room and board. She's only our landlady."

"And you won't pay room and board at Grandpa's?"

"Well, maybe after I've had time to earn some money," Audri evaded. "We have years to go, yet, to get you raised and educated, and I'm scared to spend any more of the insurance settlement than I have to. There isn't all that much of it left. Come on, Steffi, start packing your own stuff. Nothing fancy, he lives out in the sticks and runs a trailer park or something. Chances are you won't need dressy things, just jeans and shirts."

"Why can't I go with you?" Steffi's lower lip began to pooch out a little.

"I've already explained that! Nobody else will have kids along; there'd be nothing for you to do, and no one to look after you! I'll be working, and we'll probably be moving around a lot. And don't start crying, Steff, it won't work. At this point I'm all cried out myself and I have no patience for more tears."

"Eleven's too old to cry," Steffi informed her, though her eyes were stinging at the injustice of it all. "Just because Daddy died my whole world doesn't need to turn upside down, does it?"

Audri paused in exasperation. "But it does, can't you see that? Daddy's gone, there are terrible bills that weren't all covered by accident insurance, I haven't had a decent job since before he was hurt, and we're broke except for what's left of his life insurance! If this picture is a success, we'll be able to take things easier. There's always a chance a producer will spot me and see that I could fit into his future film plans and . . ."

At that point Steffi stopped listening. It was the same old pie-in-the-sky that apparently sustained her mother through all the rough places. Maybe there'd be a miracle, she'd be discovered and given a lead role instead of always playing small parts, maybe she'd get big salaries from now on, the way Daddy had. . . .

And maybe nothing would happen at all. It would be a third-rate movie, and Audri's best scenes would end up on the cutting-room floor, as usual, and Steffi would continue to take second place to whatever else was going on.

She turned away, hating the situation in which they found themselves.

It had always been Daddy who earned the big money. Stuntmen, good ones, were in short supply. Steffi had gotten used to having him laid up with broken arms or legs, with casts and bandages and bottles of pain pills sitting around. Those things were part of the price a stuntman paid to be in the business, Daddy had said. It was a fun job, a challenging one, that few other men could do, and Larry Thomas was good at it.

And then something had gone tragically wrong. The faked car wreck had become a real one, and he'd been hurt so badly that he spent nearly four months in ICU before he finally died.

Right up to the end Steffi had believed Audri's promise that he was going to recover. "He's tough," she'd said. "He'll come out of the coma, and the bones will heal, and the burns, and he'll be back to work within a few months."

But he'd never come out of the coma, and the burns had been too severe. Audri had been horrified, as well, when she was informed that her husband had exceeded his lifetime insurance benefits. Neither Steffi nor Audri Thomas were used to worrying about money at all, and now here they were, practically scraping the bottom of the barrel, trying to survive. All without the man who had kept them, most of the time, in the style to which they had all wanted to become accustomed, as he used to say.

It had taken part of the life insurance money to finish paying the medical bills. What was left seemed like a lot to Steffi, but her mother was clearly frightened about their financial future. She was economizing on even small things, like room and board here for Steffi.

It didn't look as if any of the alternatives Steffi had thought of were going to work. She was going to be stuck with spending at least a few months with a grandfather nobody else liked, who probably didn't want her any more than she wanted him.

What a bummer, Steffi thought, and kicked a chair out of the way as she passed it to lift another of the well-used suitcases onto her bed to begin packing it.

And now here she was, on a half-empty bus, rolling through the woods of Michigan, through a strange and different early summer greenery. She did recognize the white-barked birch trees, and there were a lot of some kind of pine, she thought. But mostly it was nothing like southern California.

"Place you want is right around the next bend, missy," the bus driver said over his shoulder. "They're going to meet you at the road, not pick you up in town, right?"

"I guess so," Steffi said. Her mouth was dry, and the panic that had been spreading through her middle was making a cramp in her belly.

"Here you go, then. Hidden Valley Road," the driver told her, and the bus slowed and stopped.

Steffi followed the driver out into a stillness more complete than she'd ever known. Only a faint breeze rustled the leaves around them as the man opened the bay under the bus and hauled out her bags. He set them off to the side of the road. "You sure you're going to be okay now, are you? Nobody here to meet you yet, but we're a little early. This isn't like the city, though, with a crime a minute. You're perfectly safe here, this part of the country."

"My grandpa will probably show up any minute," Steffi said, more to herself than to him.

"Okay. Good luck," he said, and a moment later she was alone with a mound of belongings, watching the bus disappear.

She stood there, motionless, for what seemed a long time. No other cars came along and she looked up at the road sign. HIDDEN VALLEY ROAD, it said. She walked a few yards closer to the beginning of the gravel road and saw the other sign, almost hidden behind the trees.

It wasn't very big, and it was so long unpainted that she could hardly read what it said. HIDDEN VALLEY TRAILER PARK. OVERNITERS WELCOME. V. TOMASCHEK, PROP.

She'd almost forgotten that her grandfather would be named Tomaschek. Before Steffi was even born, her father had changed his name from Ludwig Tomaschek to Larry Thomas. It sounded more American, was easier to pronounce and to spell, and nobody ever commented on it or took him for a foreigner, Mom said.

Well, at least this was the right place. Maybe her grandpa had misunderstood the time she was to arrive. Or he was delayed, somehow. She wondered if she should wait a while, or just start walking.

Carrying all her luggage was out of the question. She hadn't brought many clothes, but there had been favorite books she hadn't wanted put into storage with the rest of their stuff. And she didn't care if Audri did think it was childish, she'd packed her old teddy bear. He wasn't as heavy as the books, but he was kind of bulky. Steffi didn't have enough hands to pick everything up, and there was no telling how far she'd have to walk down the gravel road.

Since she had to leave part of her stuff behind, she decided to leave it all. She moved the luggage, piece by piece, well off the road and behind the trees where it was unlikely anyone would see it and steal it, just in case the bus driver was wrong about crime in the country.

The trees closed in on both sides of the road as she walked, tempering the summer heat. She tried to reassure herself that living in an RV park wouldn't be bad. She'd been in a few of them when Daddy had borrowed Steve Murphy's motorhome. Steve was a character actor, never had the big, juicy parts, but he always worked.

Steve's motorhome was one of those custom coaches that had everything from a microwave to an ice maker, a big color TV, and a tiled bathroom with a shower. It had been fun to travel in, and they'd stayed in some fancy parks. There had been swimming pools that looked like clear turquoise gems under the sun, and tennis courts, and sometimes trails where you could ride horses.

The farther she walked along the gravel road, though, the less likely it seemed that Hidden Valley was going to disclose such a park. The trees pressed in so closely on each side that Steffi doubted one of those big, high rigs could even travel this way without being scraped by the branches.

She calculated that she'd walked at least a couple of miles, and was wondering if she'd somehow missed the trailer park because it was hidden even better than its name implied, when she finally spotted something at one side of the road.

A rural mailbox. Her steps quickened until she reached a point where she could read the name, also in fading paint that was difficult to decipher.

TOMASCHEK, HIDDEN VALLEY RV PARK.

It was a relief to have found it, but it also meant that any minute now she'd be facing the grandfather who hadn't liked her mother, apparently had *hated* her father, and probably wasn't going to be overjoyed to meet *her*, either.

She was beginning to get hungry. Breakfast had been a doughnut and a cup of hot chocolate, early this morning in a bus station a long way back. Something about the sharply pine-scented air seemed to be making her appetite stronger, and she wished she'd fortified herself with a bag of peanuts or a candy bar from a vending machine at the bus station.

She'd left the gravel road. The driveway was no more than a sandy track where the trees pushed in even closer. Steffi's misgivings grew with every step. What if the place was abandoned? Deserted?

But no, that wouldn't be the case. Mom had written to the old man, telling him that Steffi was coming. All he'd had to do, if he didn't want her, was to write back and say so.

Then, Steffi thought, pulse suddenly racing as a small snake wriggled across the dirt track in front of her, she would have figured out a way to stay with Meggie. Meggie rented out rooms to boarders. She was middle-aged and fat and cheerful except when someone stiffed her for a board bill. Down-on-their-luck actors sometimes did that.

She waited until the snake disappeared into the weeds on the other side of the drive, then moved cautiously ahead.

They hadn't lived in boardinghouses when Daddy was alive. They'd had a lovely apartment, where Steffi had her own room and private bathroom. Stuntmen earned good wages, and Daddy'd never been stingy about how the money was spent. There had been that beautiful lavender bike for her eleventh birthday, the one they'd sold along with everything else that was worth anything. And clothes, she'd had enough clothes for a princess. Unfortunately she'd been in a growth spurt, and she'd outgrown a lot of the clothes. Mom hadn't wanted to spend the money to replace them until it was time to go back to school.

Mom had sold some of their clothes on consignment. That meant that when the secondhand store sold them, for far less than Audri had paid for them, they would get a share of the money. They'd hoped that would happen and they'd get at least a small check before Audri went off on location. It hadn't happened, though.

Majestic Films wasn't as grand a production company as it sounded, but the last picture her mother had done had been with them, and it hadn't been bad. Steffi had gone with her mother to see it when it first came out. *Avenger of the Pecos* had been a swashbuckling adventure and romance. Audri had played a secondary character, who had died in a shoot-out halfway through the movie. As usual, some of her best scenes had been deleted before the picture made it to the big screen, but Steffi had to admit her mother wasn't bad in the scenes that were left in.

Audri had wanted to leave after her own final scene, with a close-up of her pretty face contorted as she died. But the movie had been interesting enough so that Steffi wanted to stay through to the end, though her mother said she could tell her how it all came out.

"I want to see it," Steffi insisted. Her mother gave in and got another popcorn to last them until the credits rolled.

It wasn't fair, Steffi reflected, to have let her grow up thinking that her opinion, her needs, were important. Not if, the first time anything serious came up, everything that she thought and wanted was overruled.

She mourned the nice apartment, and the bike, and moving away from her friends at school because Meggie's place was in a different part of town. But most of all she missed Daddy.

Her best friend, Sally, had tried to comfort her. "My dad's gone, too. I know how you miss him," she'd said.

Steffi had shaken her head vigorously, denying that it was the same thing. "Your dad didn't die, he just divorced your mom. And you still see him every other Saturday. I'm never going to see *my* dad again."

It was a mistake to have allowed herself to start thinking about Daddy. Steffi's eyes blurred with tears and she could hardly see where she was going. Remembering Larry Thomas meant seeing him in a hospital bed, swathed in bandages, unmoving, unhearing, unresponsive. Mom said he probably knew they were there, even though he was unconscious, but Steffi didn't believe it. It was impossible to imagine him as a big, good-looking man who laughed a lot, and called her Steffikins as if she were a little girl, and who bought her practically everything she'd ever said she wanted.

It was a mistake, trying to walk and cry at the same time. She tripped over a large root that extended across the driveway, and landed on her hands and knees, scraping one palm on a sharp rock.

The next thing she knew, a rough warm tongue was licking at her cheek.

Steffi sat back on her heels, raising a protective arm across her face.

The dog was big and black, and his breath smelled of fish. *Rotten* fish.

"Uck," Steffi grunted. "Get down! Sit!"

Obediently the animal lowered his haunches to the ground, his tongue lolling out.

And then Steffi realized that someone was standing over them.

An old man, in threadbare jeans and a patched blue plaid shirt, looked down at her. "You lost, girl?" he asked.

She forgot about crying and the stink of the dog's breath. "I don't think so. I'm Stefanie Thomas." And then, as she evaluated the man's age, she added, "Mom said Hidden Valley RV Park. Are you my grandfather?"

2

The old man's face darkened, twisting into a frown.

Steffi's stomach twisted, too. She felt at a disadvantage, being on the ground at his feet, and she sprang up, ignoring the sore place on her hand. The dog leaped to his feet also, and licked her fingers with his fishy tongue.

It wasn't the dog that held her attention, though.

In a standing position she saw that the old man wasn't very big, not nearly as tall as her father had been. And he was almost painfully thin.

His hair showed a lot of gray among the black. He was darkly tanned, and the eyes . . . it was the eyes that convinced her of their relationship. They were an unusual brownish-green, the way Daddy's had been, the way her own were.

He hadn't said anything, so she tried again. "I'm Steffi."

His scowl carved deeper lines in his face. "Steffi," he repeated, as if the name meant nothing to him.

The hammering in her chest grew harder. "Weren't . . . weren't you expecting me? Mom wrote to you. . . ."

The answer was obvious in his expression. She wondered if he'd even known he had a granddaughter. And if he was surprised, it wasn't because he was delighted.

"She . . . she knew you didn't write letters, you didn't even answer when she wrote and told you Daddy died, so she just said to let her know if you didn't want me to come. Otherwise, she'd put me on the bus."

There was still no understanding, no welcome on the old man's face.

"We couldn't afford plane fare," Steffi said, trying not to sound as desperate and dismayed as she felt. "I came on the bus. All the way from California."

This still brought forth no reaction beyond the scowl, and she took a deep breath and told herself not to panic.

"Since Daddy's gone, we haven't had much money," she said. "Mom could only get odd jobs, a few walk-on parts. And then they offered her a bigger part, but she had to go on location somewhere in New Mexico, and she couldn't take me."

"You must have had friends in California," the old man said finally. He sounded incredulous that she had come *here*.

Steffi swallowed. "Not really. Meggie was our friend, but she couldn't afford to let me stay in a room Mom couldn't pay for. And the other people—well, they were all acquaintances, more than friends. They're all movie people, too, and nobody needed an extra kid."

His look suggested he didn't need or want one, either. What was she going to do if he refused to let her stay?

It was impossible to keep her consternation under control. She felt as if she couldn't breathe. She had to know.

"I'm sorry if you didn't get the letter. Can I stay here with you? Until my mom comes back from shooting this picture?"

"Movies," he repeated. "So they never got out of that. She's still trying to be a movie star and get rich, just like he was."

"Well, she's a pretty good actress," Steffi said. "It could happen."

"Why don't she just get a job? A real job?"

In the absence of her mother, Steffi felt she had to make some defense, even though there had been times when she'd thought the same thing herself.

"It's a job," she managed. "Like any other job. Teaching, or . . . or working in an office. She gets a pay-check for it."

"But not enough to take care of her kid."

"Not right now," Steffi admitted. The dog was still nosing around her hand, and she dropped her fingers behind his ears and scratched at them. At least the dog wasn't antagonistic. "There would have been money if the hospital bills hadn't taken it all. When she gets back on her feet, I'll be able to go home again. She couldn't work while Dad was sick, we just stayed there in the hospital with him. But she usually works."

She wished she'd never gotten off the bus, never

walked all the way in here, to meet this disagreeable old man. And for a moment she hated her mom for sending her here without being sure that Victor Tomaschek would accept her.

"Do you need proof I'm your granddaughter?" she asked. "All I have is a student ID card."

He snorted. "Don't need any ID. You're the spitting image of my son."

"So do I stay?" Steffi demanded, hoping he couldn't see that she was trembling. "Or do you want to call the police to come and get me?"

It was a challenge, and for a matter of seconds she wasn't sure he wasn't going to call her bluff. If it *was* a bluff.

"Not much of any place to put you," he grunted after a moment that went on too long. "Nobody lived in that house but me for a lot of years."

"I don't take up much space," Steffi said. Her chest was so tight it ached. How could Mom have put her in this position? Daddy never would have.

"Well, you'll have to clean out that back bedroom yourself," he offered ungraciously. "My arthritis, I'd have a busted back if I moved that junk around."

He turned and headed in the direction Steffi had been going. The dog started to follow him, then paused and looked at her, wagging his tail slightly.

Steffi didn't know much about dogs, but she thought he was a black Labrador. She decided that even though she wasn't welcome, her grandfather had indicated that he wasn't going to call the cops to haul her away, and she followed.

After only a few hundred yards, the trees receded and she was in the clearing of the Hidden Valley RV Park.

Disappointment swept over her, but at least, Steffi reminded herself, she was staying. She didn't even have a phone number where she could call her mother; the crew would be moving around too much. In an emergency she could call the Los Angeles offices of Majestic Films. Of course if her grandfather hadn't decided she could stay, that would have been an emergency, all right.

A sign—OFFICE—hung over the porch steps to the main building. It was more a rustic cabin than a house, by Steffi's reckoning. It was toward that that Victor Tomaschek headed, and she followed, keeping one hand on the big dog's head. It was silky soft and oddly comforting to her touch.

There was no lawn, only a little straggly grass that had mostly been beaten down. Off to the left, across from the office, stood a swimming pool, but it was no turquoise jewel. The water was a scummy dark green, as if it had stood there for a long time, unused. Not far from it was a large propane tank.

The road, or rather the sandy track, wound on between pool and office, through the trees. She caught glimpses of small trailers and an ancient-looking motorhome, nothing like the ones she had seen in the classy parks. An elderly lady in a flowered housedress was walking a little dog, and she paused to glance curiously at Steffi.

The track made a loop off each side of the center drive, with trailer spaces at irregular intervals. From the far end of it a path continued on deeper into the woods, where there was a glimpse of blue. A lake? Cleaner water, at any rate, than what was in the pool.

The dog started to follow Steffi inside when her

grandfather pulled open the screen door, but its master turned and spoke sharply. "Stay, Buddy. You went and got in them rotten fish that kid was supposed to have buried, and you stink too much to come inside."

Buddy's tail wavered, then sank between his legs as he lowered himself flat on the decking of the porch and looked up with mournful brown eyes.

"See you later, Buddy," Steffi said under her breath, and was rewarded with a single thump of the black tail.

To the right, as she entered the hallway that ran from front to back of the small building, was an office and limited store. Bread, milk, a few canned goods, Steffi noticed. A counter with a cash register. There was a pay phone just inside the front door.

The other side of the hallway was where they were going. This part of the house was living space.

A small room was sparsely furnished with a couch and one recliner, a tabletop TV, and a surprisingly large bookcase, crammed to overflowing. Beyond that, there was a kitchen the same size as the living room. Old-fashioned, orderly except for a cup and saucer on a linoleum-covered counter. No dishwasher. No microwave, no ice maker, no freezer except for an upper compartment on the refrigerator.

There were two bedrooms, the smaller of which her grandfather waved her into. "Been nothing but a storage place for years. I got to get back to work." With that, he left her there.

Steffi stood for a moment in the doorway, biting her lip.

"Welcome to Hidden Valley," she said aloud. Behind her, on the other side of the screen, Buddy whined. "Sorry," she called to him. "My grandpa thinks you stink." That reminded her that he'd licked her hand. That, too, smelled fishy, so she went into the bathroom to wash.

The bath was as out-of-date as the rest of the place. Reasonably clean, though certainly not spotless, it was sort of an off-white, with a basin on a pedestal and a tub on clawed feet. Even the towels were off-white, adding to the drab effect.

Her stomach growled, reminding her that it was well past lunchtime. Her grandfather hadn't invited her to eat, but she was going to, anyway, if she could find anything.

Back to the kitchen, then, before she tackled that storage room she was supposed to sleep in. For a moment she felt a flare of resentment as she imagined her mother, in a trailer owned by Majestic Films, with all the modern conveniences. She supposed she was lucky there was a bathroom; after the rest of the place, she wouldn't have been surprised if there had been an outhouse.

The refrigerator and the cupboard nearest to it yielded lunch meat and bread and mayonnaise. There were canned goods, peas and carrots and green beans and sliced peaches. She opened the fruit, and because it was a small can, she ate the entire contents.

There was an outside door from the kitchen, too, which looked out over the back part of the park and the woods. From here she could see the lake. And Buddy, giving up on the front door, had come around to the back. He pushed his nose against the screen, begging to be let in.

"I don't know how to make you smell better," Steffi told him. "Here, have the crusts off my sandwich." She opened the door a crack to hand them to him, only to have him gratefully lick her hand again. "Now see what you've done. Where did you find the rotten fish?"

The voice startled her. "I thought I buried it deep enough, but old Buddy's a digger. Sorry about that."

The speaker was a boy who had just come around the corner of the building. Tall, skinny, in ragged jeans and a shrunken T-shirt, he was probably about twelve. He had brown hair and blue eyes, and freckles across his nose. Steffi had never cared for freckles, but just those few were rather appealing.

"Who're you?" the boy asked.

"Steffi. Thomas. I'm . . . Mr. Tomaschek is my grandfather."

"No kidding. I thought any relative of his would have horns and one eye in the middle of his forehead." He paused, assessing her through the fine wire mesh of the door, then added, "I'm Casey Chapman. You just visiting?"

"Until I can go back to California to be with my mom. She's on location in New Mexico right now, making a movie."

"She's a movie star?" Respect showed on the boy's face.

"Well, not a star, actually. More of a bit player, mostly, but she has the second lead in this one. *Smoke Signals West.*"

"Cowboys and Indians?" Casey guessed.

"Right. Mom says Westerns are coming back."

"Never replace science fiction, I hope. I'm supposed to haul away the garbage can. Put it out where the truck can pick it up."

"Is it inside?" Steffi asked, looking around.

"No, right over there behind the house. And there's one in the laundry room, too."

"Where's that?" Steffi wanted to know. She'd probably have to do her own laundry; she guessed the old man wasn't going to wait on her much.

"You want to come look at it? It's at the far end of the hall from the front door."

It seemed reasonable to get oriented, and maybe this Casey could help her with the heavier boxes in the back bedroom. He certainly had more muscles than she did.

She followed him across the rear of the building to the door into the laundry room. It was cramped and had several flies trapped in the single window, buzzing in frustration.

There were two washing machines, one with an OUT OF ORDER sign on it, and one large dryer. A table for folding clothes, a rack for hangers, a wastebasket.

Not much like the gleaming rows of washers and dryers Steffi had seen in other campgrounds.

She turned as a woman hurried along the corridor past the open doorway, then stopped and returned when she realized Steffi and Casey were in the laundry room. Steffi recognized the flowered dress; it was the woman who had been walking the little dog. She was very thin and had gray hair that seemed not to have been combed too recently.

"Don't tell them you've seen me," she urged, lowering her voice dramatically. "If they ask, I've moved out, and you don't know where I've gone."

Then she vanished out the back door. Through the window, Steffi saw her hurrying along a pathway into the woods.

"What was that all about?" Steffi wondered.

"That's Mrs. Risku. Helen. She's almost ninety. Every time anybody new shows up, she hides."

Steffi stared at him in astonishment. "Why? What's she afraid of?"

Casey shrugged, hauling the wastebasket out to dump it into the larger garbage can outside. "I don't know. She seems to think somebody's after her. She talks to herself. I hear her when I walk past her trailer. Dad says lots of people who live alone talk to themselves."

"What're they supposed to do?" The angry-sounding voice came from the doorway they'd just come out of, and Steffi jumped and turned to face her grandfather. "A person have to be mute just because she lives alone?"

"No. No, sir." Casey hoisted the big black can over his shoulder and started around the corner with it.

Steffi hesitated, glancing toward the woods where the old woman had disappeared. "Is she . . . all right?" she ventured.

"She's just old, not batty. Pays her trailer space rent on time. That's all that matters to me." The old man continued to sound fierce.

"Umm. Uh, I hope it was okay, I made myself something to eat."

"That's what I came to tell you. Forgot it was past noon. Sometimes I don't remember to eat on schedule."

He turned to retreat into the building, and Steffi stopped him. "Ah, am I supposed to call you Grandpa, or what?"

For a few seconds she thought something flickered in his face, some reaction new to him, perhaps. He grunted. "Name's Victor. You can call me Vic." With that he stumped away, letting the screen door bang behind him.

Well, she thought, was that supposed to put me in my place? No family relationship? He'd disowned her father, and now he was denying any words that might suggest he was her grandfather?

She'd gone through her life so far with no relatives except her parents. So she wasn't any worse off, was she, if the old man didn't want to acknowledge kinship? Why, then, did she feel hurt?

Steffi walked around the house rather than through it, following Casey, hoping he hadn't already gone home. She wanted to ask for his help.

She found him talking to a man in a camper, parked beside the propane tank. Was this the someone new here, someone Mrs. Risku was afraid of?

Steffi inspected the newcomer, an older man in worn clothes. There was some kind of fishing lure with red feathers tucked under the band around his hat. Why would an old woman be afraid of him?

"I'll have to get Mr. Tomaschek to pump your propane," Casey was saying. "I'm not allowed to do that."

"All right. You got today's newspapers?"

"No. Sorry. All the regulars here get theirs delivered in a tube out by the highway. Whoever comes in after they're left there brings them in, usually, but they don't come until about four o'clock. I'll get Vic to get the propane for you."

Casey started toward the front door, saw Steffi, and nodded as if they were acquaintances, at least. Not enemies. She was afraid that was the way Vic saw her. As unwelcome as his son, her father, had been.

Why? she wondered. What could her father possibly have done to him? Daddy had always been great to *her*.

She leaned against one of the posts at the foot of the steps, watching her grandfather come out and head toward the waiting camper. Casey followed, and she stopped him.

"Are you working for my . . . for Vic? Are you busy?"

"I've done all I need to do for now. I sort of work for him, but he doesn't pay me. We just get a special rate on our rent. I do a few of the things Vic doesn't want to do. He says my bones are younger than his."

Steffi was baffled. "What's that mean?"

"Means he's got arthritis pretty bad. He hurts a lot of the time. Makes him grouchy. Short-tempered. It bothers him to lift things like the garbage cans, or dig holes to bury fish guts, or sweep off the porch. Stuff like that. But I guess I'm finished for today."

"I thought maybe you'd be willing to help me move some stuff. Boxes, mostly. I have to clear out the back bedroom and make a place to sleep."

"Oh, okay. Where you going to put the boxes?" Casey, at least, was amiable. Maybe it did make a person short-tempered if he was hurting all the time, Steffi conceded.

"I don't know. There're quite a few of them."

It took them well over an hour to clear out the room so there was enough space to move around in. Casey went out and asked Vic if they could store most of the stuff in a shed out back, and then they had to rearrange the things that were already there to make room.

They had to leave a few cartons in the bedroom, but it looked a lot better. It wasn't until they'd found sheets and made up the bed that Steffi remembered her luggage.

"I left it out by the road, behind some trees. There was too much to carry so far. I hope nobody stole it."

"Not likely," Casey said cheerfully. "Hasn't been a crime worse than spitting on a sidewalk since I got here."

"How long's that been?" Steffi asked.

"Three months."

"Did you have to change schools, then? Did you go in town?"

For just a moment Casey hesitated. "Well, no. I just finished out the year working with my dad, at home. It didn't seem worthwhile to register in a new school for such a short time. Listen, don't worry about your suitcases. When my dad comes home, we can probably take the pickup out to the highway and get them."

"Thanks," Steffi told him, genuinely grateful.

"Okay. See you later," Casey said, and flipped a hand at her as he left.

She could hear Vic and someone else in the store across the hall, and she wondered if he'd forget to eat supper, too. It was a quarter to six, and her stomach was beginning to rumble again. There hadn't been much in the refrigerator, and it dawned on her that her grandfather wasn't exactly prepared to feed a kid; he didn't seem to have much even for himself.

That became more evident when supper finally was put on the kitchen table. Canned hash, bread and butter, and more fruit out of a can.

"Have to get some groceries next time I get to town," Vic said as they sat down. "Ain't bought anything in a couple of weeks. I don't carry much at the store, no market for it. People mostly shop in town except for bread and milk."

The meal was simple, yet it smelled good. He might not want her there, but he was speaking to her, Steffi thought. She picked up her fork and lifted it full of hash, only to realize that Vic was bowing his head, saying grace.

Embarrassed, she hoped he hadn't noticed that she'd already started to eat, and waited until he'd finished. It made her feel peculiar, that this grumpy old man was expressing thanks for their food.

She ate everything on her plate and found herself wishing there was just a little bit more. When they had finished, Steffi hesitated. Mom had told her to pitch in and do her share, so she made the offer. "You want me to wash the dishes?"

He met her gaze. "Wouldn't mind. I can watch the news."

It only took a few minutes to wash a couple of plates and some silverware. When she moved into the living room where Vic sat in the recliner watching the TV, she saw that it was black and white.

She'd never seen a black-and-white TV set except in old movies. So much for life in the sticks.

The reporter on the screen was talking about the latest presidential fight with Congress, and then about a possible strike coming up with the phone company employees, and then about missing kids. The photos of two little girls appeared, so dark and smudgy she could hardly make them out. Even for a set without color, this one seemed pretty pathetic.

As soon as the news ended, Vic turned off the set and picked up a newspaper. That reminded Steffi that maybe Casey had gotten his dad to bring her luggage. Without it she didn't have anything to sleep in.

Vic didn't seem to notice when she wandered outside. It was cooling off, and there were a few mosquitoes. She wished Mom had thought of packing insect repellent.

There were lights coming on in some of the trailers and the antique motorhome, which was set way in the back, almost hidden in the pines. Several cars and pickups that hadn't been there earlier were now parked in among the trees.

Steffi started walking along the road that bisected the loop where the parking spaces were. They called this an RV park, but with the exception of the camper driven by the man who had bought propane, these weren't recreational vehicles. People were living in them. Permanently, it seemed, judging by the awnings, boots, bikes, and storage units around the rigs.

Most of them were really small, smaller than the trailer she knew would be provided for her mom on location. A whole family appeared to live in one no more than twenty feet long: parents, two preschoolers, and a toddler. They were eating their evening meal at a picnic table surrounded by hanging lights so yellow Steffi thought they were designed to repel bugs. She wondered how they could all sleep in the trailer. No wonder they were eating outside. What did they do when it rained, or when it was winter?

Steffi felt a wave of homesickness. Not only for her mother, but for Daddy, who was gone forever, and for a home of her own. Of course the apartment they'd had while they were still a family hadn't really been their own *house*. But they'd planned to buy a little ranch somewhere out in the valley, big enough so Steffi could maybe have a horse. They'd talked about doing it when Mom hit it big as an actress, or Daddy saved up enough money. Actually, he'd had quite a bit put aside for it, before the accident that had swallowed up all the savings. They'd cut pictures out of *Architectural Digest,* photographs of palatial homes, and rustic ranch houses, and seaside cottages. There had been swimming pools and tennis courts and all the things they joked about wanting.

One of Daddy's hobbies had been cooking, so they saved pictures of big fancy kitchens, too. Many a happy Sunday he and Steffi had spent the day dicing and slicing and chopping, making sauces, roasting, broiling, stir-frying whatever they'd found fresh at the market. Audri wasn't all that keen on doing the work, but she'd always appreciated their efforts and eaten heartily, and she'd set an elegant table to showcase whatever they fixed.

Steffi blinked against the threatening tears, wondering if she'd ever get over losing her father. She didn't think so.

It was hard to realize that Vic had been *her dad's* father.

Why hadn't *they* liked each other, done things together? It was impossible to figure out.

Steffi swatted at a mosquito and read the homemade sign in front of the little trailer where the family lived. THE MONTONIS, it said. It was bright and colorful. Each person's name was in a different color. Frank and Carol, Danny, Jenny, and Gus.

The eaters looked up and smiled. A boy about four—Danny or Gus?—said, "Hi."

"Hi," Steffi replied, envying the little family. They were together, even if they did have to live in a tiny trailer.

The lady in the flowered dress, Mrs. Risku, lived in the trailer across the road from the Montonis. She was watching her little dog, who was digging around the base of a tree. He looked up to bark at Steffi.

"No, no, Barkley. This young lady is not a stranger. You must be nice to her." Mrs. Risku smiled at Steffi. "Are you Vic's granddaughter? He didn't tell us you were coming."

Barkley came over to investigate. He couldn't reach her fingers, the way Buddy could, so he leaped around her legs in excitement at having a visitor.

"He didn't know," Steffi admitted, pausing. She didn't know whether to pet Barkley or not. "My mom sent a letter, but he never got it."

She was only beginning to comprehend what a catastrophe her arrival might be for her grandfather. Her mother had always told her to mind her manners, to be considerate of other people, but this hadn't been considerate. It wasn't right to have sent a letter and not waited for a reply before putting Steffi on a bus and sending her here. It wasn't even a good enough excuse that Vic hadn't replied to any previous attempt at communication. It was mortifying, when Steffi thought about it. It was a lot of nerve to intrude on someone who obviously didn't want her.

Vic had been unwelcoming. As he'd had a perfect right to be. And now she was stuck with him, and he with her. Steffi thought of a number of things she'd say to her mother when she saw her next.

"Barkley likes you," Mrs. Risku told her, smiling. She seemed perfectly normal now. "What is your name, dear?"

Steffi told her. "And you're Mrs. Risku, Casey said."

"Oh, call me Helen. Everybody calls me Helen. Except my daughter Eunice. She calls me Mother." She laughed and shook her head. "Isn't it strange, when I named her, I thought Eunice was a lovely name." The smile changed to a frown. "Now I can hardly bear it. I wonder if I stopped liking the name when I stopped liking my daughter?"

Steffi didn't know what to say to that. She smiled weakly. "I'm just out for a walk. I hoped I'd find Casey; he said his dad might bring in my luggage from where I had to leave it."

"Casey? He's a nice boy, isn't he? He brings Barkley bones and scraps. I don't eat much meat anymore. Can't chew well enough, you know, unless the meat is ground up. I'm glad you're here, dear. You'll cheer up your grandpa."

Steffi didn't have any response to that, either, since she doubted the truth of the statement. She was glad when Mrs. Risku—no, Helen (was it all right to call such an old lady by her first name?)—volunteered the information that Casey lived right next door to her.

"He's not there right now, though. I saw him walking out toward the road. Maybe he went to meet his father. The poor man is awfully late coming home from work. He works in town, you know, at the Moon Bay Supermarket. Moon Bay isn't a very big town, but it has a good market. Of course I don't need to buy much these days, for just Barkley and me."

Steffi looked down at the little dog, who had finally stopped leaping all over her and was staring up at her expectantly. It dawned on her that he might be waiting for a treat.

"I'm sorry," she said. "I don't have a dog biscuit or anything."

"Oh, he's such a beggar! Don't pay any attention to him."

"He's . . . unusual looking, isn't he?" Steffi felt compelled to comment.

"Yes, isn't he cute?" Helen beamed fondly at the animal.

"Umm," Steffi murmured. At close range, she thought Barkley was about the ugliest little mutt she'd ever seen. His hair was so short and so white that from a slight distance he looked almost like a pig, with pink skin showing through the hair. There was one brown spot, the size of a man's hand, on his rump, and three more on his head and face that made him look like a clown. "Umm, hi, Barkley."

Barkley sat up on his hind legs, lifted tiny paws into the air, and barked.

"I don't know what I'd do without Barkley. He's been my friend and companion for, oh, almost fifteen years now," Helen said. Then, for some reason, what seemed like distress crossed her face, though it quickly faded. Steffi wondered if she'd had an unexpected pain.

They both turned at the sound of an approaching vehicle. It was a camper, with two people in the cab. "Is that Casey's father?" Steffi asked. But when she turned toward the old lady, Helen was hurrying away, with Barkley close on her heels. The woman hadn't even excused herself.

"Anytime someone new shows up," Casey had said, "she hides."

How peculiar. So the people in the camper were strangers, but there was a dark blue pickup right behind them, raising a cloud of dust. It drew up alongside the camper, and when Casey stepped out of the pickup, Steffi walked quickly to meet him.

Just before she reached the porch, where her luggage was being unloaded, she glanced back.

There was no sign of Helen or Barkley. Had they entered the trailer, or gone off into the woods again?

How peculiar, Steffi thought again. Did Helen really have a reason to be afraid of someone, or had she simply gotten a bit odd in her old age?

Casey's dad was big and good-looking in a rough-hewn way. He acknowledged Casey's introduction with a nod. "Be good for Vic to have you here," he said.

Why did everyone think she would be good for Vic? So far he wasn't particularly good for *her*, though if he'd refused to let her stay it would have been far worse.

Mr. Chapman unloaded the last of her luggage and drove on back to his trailer, leaving his son to carry it all inside for Steffi.

Vic glanced up when they went through the living room, but he didn't say anything. When Casey had brought in the last load, he lingered just inside Steffi's bedroom.

"There's still a lot of junk in here," Casey observed, looking at the stack of boxes across one end of the room.

"I think it would all fit in the shed out back if Vic would let us haul some of the stuff that's already in there to the dump. Shall I ask him?"

"It would be nice to have the space. This is an awfully small room," Steffi agreed.

She heard their murmuring voices in the living room as she put each bag on her bed and unpacked it, hanging clothes in the closet or putting them into the dresser. She couldn't tell what Vic's reaction was.

She emerged from her bedroom in time to hear a vehicle drive into the campground, and she went to a window to look out as her grandfather moved across the hall to the office.

Another pickup with a camper, this one with an Indiana license plate and a small boat on the top of it. A man got out and came up the steps, a man of forty, maybe, with red hair and a blue baseball cap, a dark green T-shirt, and faded jeans.

Vic had left the doors open between the living quarters and the office, and Steffi could hear their voices clearly.

"Evening," Vic grunted.

"Evening. Heard there was some good fishing out there in the lake," the newcomer said.

"Need a Michigan license," Vic said.

"Just happen to have picked one up. You have space for my rig?"

"I reckon. You want water, electric, and sewer? Or just parking space?"

"Better give me all three," the man said. Steffi moved so that she could see him as he stood at the counter in the office. Her grandfather had pulled out a form and picked up a pen.

"How many nights?" he asked.

The baseball cap was pushed back as the man scratched his head. "Well, tonight, anyway. Do I have to decide now? If the fishing's any good, maybe I'll stay a week or so."

"Cheaper by the week, but you can decide a day at a time if you want. Name?"

"Kurt Vail. You need my license number, right?"

Mr. Vail handed over the cash for one night, asked for a loaf of bread and a quart of milk, hesitated, then added a couple of Eskimo Pies to the assortment on the counter. "Any TV reception here?"

"One station. Don't come in very good, though."

"Go out in the sticks and you give up the niceties of civilization, eh? Okay. You need to see my fishing license?"

"Nope," Vic replied. "That's between you and the game warden. You can park in space two, right up front on the left."

"Can I drive closer to the lake, to launch my boat?"

"Straight through the middle of the park. Nobody's driven down there with a car since we opened this spring, so the road's overgrown."

Mr. Vail accepted the sack with his small store of groceries and turned to leave. "My rig's already banged up. A few more scratches won't hurt anything. Thanks."

He came out into the hall, saw Steffi, nodded and said "Hi," on his way out. Just as he reached the outer door, Steffi caught a movement in the shadows at the opposite end of the hall, and turned in time to see Helen Risku duck into the laundry room.

Hiding again? Steffi wondered. She walked toward

the woman and found her hovering just inside the doorway, out of sight.

"Who is he?" Helen wanted to know.

"He said his name is Kurt Vail. From Indiana. With a fishing license," Steffi told her. "Just a vacationer."

"That's what he says," Helen muttered, poking at her bird's nest hair that was falling into her eyes. "If he asks you any questions about me, you don't know anything, all right?"

"That would be the truth," Steffi said.

"And don't mention Barkley. By name, I mean. I couldn't change his name, you see, or he'd have been confused."

"All right," Steffi agreed, feeling confused herself.

"Nobody," Helen said fiercely, "is going to separate Barkley and me."

She went over to the dryer and unloaded a few clothes into a plastic basket, then left with them. Through the rear door, not out the front.

Steffi stared after her. Did she really think every stranger was after her *dog?* That ugly yappy little beast?

Vic was still doing something in the office. As Steffi reached the doorway, he spoke to her.

"If you want to make out a grocery list, what you want to eat, Mr. Chapman will bring it home tomorrow night. He's assistant manager of the supermarket. I got a charge account there."

"Oh. Thank you," Steffi said, surprised that he was going to let her choose her own groceries. She found paper and a pencil in the kitchen and checked out the cupboards and the refrigerator, then made her list. She guessed she was supposed to deliver the list to Casey's dad, so she went out the back and headed for the Chapman's trailer.

The newcomer had parked his rig and was hooking it up. He paused as Steffi approached.

"Nice weather, isn't it? Think it'll stay this way for a while?"

"I don't know. I just got here, and I haven't heard a weather report."

He was smiling. "You here on vacation?"

Steffi thought if she were on vacation, the Hidden Valley RV Park would probably be the last place she'd have chosen for it. "I'm staying with my grandfather for a while," she said. There was something about his smile that made her uneasy. Maybe Helen's paranoia was catching. "Excuse me. I have to deliver something."

There was no sign of Helen or Barkley when she passed their trailer. Steffi wondered if the old lady had managed to get inside without being seen by the newcomer. Did she hide until each of the overnighters had left, or what?

There was the smell of broiling hamburgers as she approached the small trailer where the Chapmans lived. With onions, Steffi decided, and even though she wasn't hungry, her mouth watered.

Both Casey and his father, Bo, were outside. Bo was turning burgers on a grill, and Casey was setting the picnic table with paper plates, catsup, and mustard.

Steffi handed over the list and explained her errand. Bo Chapman nodded and put the list in his shirt pocket. "I'll bring this stuff tomorrow night," he agreed. "You want a burger, Steffi?"

"Oh, no, I just ate a little while ago," she said quickly.

Casey's dad grinned. "Ten minutes ago would be long enough for Casey to be hungry again. Fix her a plate, son. There's plenty."

And so, though it was a bit embarrassing, Steffi accepted a thick juicy burger with everything on it, and a can of Coke fresh out of an ice chest.

Through the open doorway of the trailer she could see a foldout couch, and she wondered if Casey slept on it. Their living quarters were even more cramped than hers.

She chewed and swallowed before she spoke again. "Is the campground only open in the summer?"

"Technically." Casey offered her an open bag of corn chips. "A few people stay here over the winter. Vic doesn't take overnighters after the snow falls, I guess, but he lives here year round, so he lets anybody stay who wants to. The Montonis move into town, Burt says, but Helen stays. Sometimes they get snowed in for a few days, but the county snowplow comes in as far as the mailbox, so Vic keeps his truck out there for emergencies."

The hamburger was delicious. Steffi took a swig of Coke and asked, "Who's Burt?"

"He's the kid who lives in the last trailer on this side, way at the back closest to the lake. Burt Taylor and his dad, Chester. Burt's sixteen. He works in town at a gas station. His dad's on disability or something, hurt his back on some job, so he doesn't work. They stayed here all winter last year."

"Are there any other kids? Besides the little Montoni ones?"

"Nope. That's it. And Burt doesn't consider himself a kid. Not like us, anyway. So don't expect him to be any company for you."

Steffi considered that. "What do you do to keep busy, then?"

"I do odd jobs for Vic. Fish a little, when I can borrow a boat."

"Swim?"

"No. The lake's ice cold, and there's no beach. Just rocks that kill your feet."

"How about the pool?"

Casey's eyebrows rose. "Have you looked in it? Green slime!"

"Couldn't it be cleaned out?"

Casey thought about it. "Be an awful lot of work."

Bo heaped raw onions onto his second burger. "What else do you have to do? Might be a good project, to get the pool usable again. You always used to like to swim."

"If my grandfather says it's okay, would you help me do it?" Steffi proposed.

Casey shot a look at his father. "Would you help, too, Dad? Just with the worst of it?"

"Like getting rid of the green slime? Well, maybe, if you kids would scrub it down and maybe repaint it. I think it'll need paint."

Steffi walked back to the main house feeling a little better after she'd finished her second supper. Maybe, if they got the pool fixed up, it wouldn't be quite so boring around here. There'd be something to do until she could go home. And then she thought, with a pang, that there no longer was a place to call home.

Up ahead, she saw Kurt Vail sitting in a lawn chair in front of his pickup and camper. He was watching her, and though she couldn't have said why that bothered her,

Steffi changed her mind about walking past him. She didn't want to talk to him again. She turned suddenly and cut through the space between two of the trailers, as if she wanted to walk in the woods instead.

"I'm getting as nutty as Helen Risku," she muttered as she took one of the paths that meandered all around the area.

This one headed out toward the lake, so she followed it, although it was dusk now and the mosquitoes were in fine form. She was glad she didn't have as much trouble with them as her mom did, or she'd have red lumps all over her. Daddy had always said his skin was too tough for them to penetrate, and she hoped her skin was that way, too.

It was only a short distance to the edge of the water. Casey was right about the rocks. They'd be hard to walk on, and it wasn't a good place to swim.

She tried going a little way along the shore, but after turning her ankle on the stones, she gave up. She'd take the short way back, on the main trail right through the middle of the camp. And if Kurt Vail was still there, well, to heck with him, she'd just walk past him. She didn't have to talk to him if she didn't want to.

There were male voices coming from the first trailer she reached. This would be the "last" one at the back of the park, and it was the smallest and shabbiest one she'd seen yet.

It was getting dark in among the trees, and there was a light on inside the trailer. The voices got louder as she came alongside it, and they were angry, or at least one of them was.

"Stupid doggone kid, you try anything like that again and I'll break your neck," a man said.

Steffi hesitated, startled, then began to walk more quickly. The man sounded nasty.

A response came in a younger-sounding voice. "All right, then, do it all yourself. But don't yell at me because *you're* the one that's stupid!"

And then, to Steffi's alarm, there was the sound of a blow, and a cry of pain or fury.

The profanity that followed after her as she hurried away was shocking and frightening.

Burt Taylor and his father, Chester. She remembered the names Casey had said.

Why were they fighting? Were they like this all the time?

She forgot about avoiding the newest camper, which was fine, because he was across the road now talking to Mr. Montoni. Neither man noticed when she walked past them.

Just as she reached the front porch, another vehicle drove in, slowly, engine rattling and gasping. A young couple, this time, with a woman carrying a baby.

Surely Helen wouldn't be afraid of this trio, would she?

She'd wait, Steffi decided, until Vic had checked them in, and then she'd ask him about fixing up the swimming pool.

Instinctively, she glanced toward the parking spaces. There was no sign of Helen or Barkley, but Kurt Vail stood beside his rig, watching the activity at the office.

Uncomfortable without knowing why, Steffi turned away and walked inside.

5

Going to sleep in a strange room was not easy. Steffi wondered if her father had slept here once, a long time ago. If the room had been his, there were no traces now of his presence. No trophies or pennants or pictures, none of the kinds of things he'd had in his study in the apartment, like the mask from Africa, or the jade elephant someone had brought him from India, or the big, heavily illustrated books. Of course as a boy he couldn't have afforded those things, but there was nothing at all here now to remind her of her father.

The bed felt funny, there was a sort of musty smell, and for some reason Steffi felt as if someone were moving around, just outside. Once she even got up and looked out the window.

There was a yard light over between the pool and the propane tank, so it wasn't really dark out there. Nothing stirred in the shadows around the edges of the circle of light.

Steffi was returning to bed when the sense of a presence in the room became very strong. She stopped, certain that someone was breathing only a few yards away.

She froze, listening. Yes, there were faint sounds she couldn't identify, only that they were close to her.

When Buddy's cold nose touched her hand, Steffi nearly screamed. And then she recognized him, from the lingering odor of rotten fish.

She kept her voice low so that her grandfather wouldn't hear her from the room on the other side of the bathroom. "You scared me to death," she murmured to the dog. "How come you're in here?"

He nuzzled her more firmly, and she willingly patted his smooth soft head. "Okay, you're in. But you're not sleeping with me, not with your bad breath. I put a rag rug down on the floor; you can sleep on that," she told him.

He seemed to understand when she instructed him to lie down beside her bed. And with Buddy there, she stopped worrying about noises and drifted off to sleep.

When she approached Vic the next day about the swimming pool, he stared at her. "Not that simple," he said.

Steffi's mouth was dry. "Can't we just get the dirty water out of it and refill it?"

"Take more than that. Pump will empty it, all right. I emptied it out last fall like I was supposed to, but the tarp blew off, and it snowed in there. I hooked things up so we could use the pool water for fighting a fire if we ever had one," he said. "We're too far out for a hydrant, and this makes my insurance lower. I'll turn on the pump when I get the chance. But there's chemicals have to go in it, it has to be tested regular to be sure. Can't use it, otherwise. And I don't know if I have time to keep up with that."

"Couldn't we learn to do that part of it? The testing? Casey and I?" She really wanted that pool.

Vic considered for so long she was afraid he was going to say no. Then he grunted. "Suppose so," he said, and walked away.

Steffi was surprised at his cooperation, even given as it was in what seemed a gruff and grudging manner. She was relieved that they weren't going to have to stand in the slimy water and bail it out by hand.

Casey showed up within minutes of the time the pump went on. He stood watching the water level drop, and grinned across at Steffi. "Looks like we're going to have a place to swim. Do you think we ought to paint it, Vic, before we fill it with clean water?"

The old man stared down into the pool. "Needs scrubbing, but I don't think it has to be painted. There's scrub brushes in the shed, hanging on the wall. The testing kit and the chemical stuff are on that top shelf. But first you have to scrub it clean."

Scrubbing. Steffi and Casey exchanged glances. It looked like an awful job. Even when the water had been pretty well pumped out onto the ground a short distance away, there was a lot of sludge left.

Steffi was afraid the boy would decide it was too much work, but he didn't. When Vic turned off the pump,

Casey said, "Well, let's scoop up the rest of that crud and then get out the scrub brushes, okay?"

They worked hard at it for several hours as the sun rose higher and warmer in the sky. Down inside the pale aqua walls it got hot enough so that sweat ran down their faces and made their clothes stick to their bodies.

Everybody who came along stopped to watch and comment. There was no sign of Helen Risku or Barkley, but just about everybody else showed up.

Mrs. Montoni was there with her children, the smallest one in a stroller. "Oh, good, we're going to be able to swim. That gate will be kept closed, though, won't it? So the kids can't wander in accidentally?"

"No kids inside the fence without an adult," Casey told her, pausing to wipe his forehead with the back of his hand.

Once when a shadow fell across her, Steffi looked up to see a big burly man scowling down at her.

"Whaddya doin'?" he asked.

Steffi thought it was a silly question, but she answered politely enough. "Cleaning the pool so it can be refilled and we can use it."

"Who're you?" he wanted to know.

Casey spoke up from the other side end of the wall. "This is Steffi, Vic's granddaughter. Steffi, this is Chester Taylor."

The man who'd been yelling at his kid last night, Steffi thought. And hitting him, if she'd correctly interpreted what she'd overheard. She didn't need his antagonistic manner to know that she didn't like him.

Chester grunted. He smiled then, but it didn't make

him look much more pleasant. "Steffi, huh? Well, maybe we'll all take a dip tonight, eh?"

"Maybe not that soon," Casey guessed. "Unless everyone else wants to pitch in and help scrub the gook off the walls."

Chester Taylor lifted a hand in protest. "Don't look at me. I got a bad back. The doctors don't let me do nothing heavy, or I'd lose my disability."

Most of the people who came to inspect their work went away quickly once Casey suggested they might help.

"Sort of like *The Little Red Hen*," Steffi said. "Everybody was willing to eat whatever she cooked, but nobody was willing to do any of the work."

"Right," Casey agreed, and returned to scouring.

Kurt Vail wandered over when he came back from his morning fishing excursion. He lingered longer than the others had, asking questions, being friendly.

Too friendly? Steffi wondered. Most middle-aged men weren't that interested in a couple of kids.

"I'm getting as paranoid as Mrs. Risku," she said when he'd finally left. "Do you see anything suspicious about him?"

Instead of laughing at her, Casey leaned on the long-handled scrub brush and considered the matter. "He seems nosy. Some people are, wanting to know things that are none of their business. I don't know if that's suspicious or not. What ulterior motive could he have, wanting to know about everybody in the campground?"

Neither of them could answer that, and they went on with their labors.

It was well past noon when they broke for lunch and a much needed rest. Vic was having tea and toast with jam when Steffi entered the kitchen. She eyed it with dismay. Was that all that was available?

No, there was one rather dried slice of lunch meat to put between layers of bread. She put mayonnaise on it and decided it wasn't too bad. She was glad Mr. Chapman was bringing more stuff tonight, though.

The couple with the baby left while Steffi was having lunch. Kurt Vail asked about bait, and was directed to a shop in Moon Bay. Steffi felt oddly better after he'd gone off to find it, and foolish for being relieved when the man wasn't around.

There being no dishes to wash up, Steffi went back to work on the pool and found Casey had already begun again.

Once Kurt Vail had left camp, Helen Risku showed up. Barkley was with her, peering over the edge of the pool and barking once, just to let them know he noticed them.

"You'll keep the gate closed, won't you, so Barkley won't accidentally fall in?"

"I think he could swim," Casey assured her. "But yes, we'll keep the gate closed and latched so nobody but big people can open it. Shall we let you know when it's ready to swim in?"

"Me? Swimming? I don't think I've been swimming in fifty years or more. Mr. Risku—my husband, you know, been gone for nearly twenty years—he used to be a swimmer. We swam together when we were young. Did I ever tell you we went to Finland on our honeymoon? Swam there, off the island where he grew up. Did you know Risku is a Finnish name?"

She chattered on and on, far longer than the others

had, but for some reason that didn't bother Steffi. Helen seemed a harmless old woman.

And then, at the distant sound of an engine as some vehicle turned off the main road and came nearer, Helen and Barkley vanished.

Off to hide from strangers again, Steffi thought.

Whoever it was didn't come into the campground but went on past the driveway.

After a few more hours under what was by this time a broiling sun, Steffi was ready to quit. But Casey showed no sign of stopping, and she was ashamed, after she'd solicited his help, to be the first to admit to being bushed.

Finally, though, Casey threw down his brush and announced, "I need something cold to drink. You want to go get a Pepsi?"

He didn't have to ask her twice.

That whole day Buddy followed her around, watching her with such mournful eyes that Casey teased her. "You've got an admirer, looks like. He's never paid that much attention to anyone else."

Even when Vic went off to tend to something, Buddy stayed with Steffi. And now that his fishy breath was no longer quite so strong, Vic didn't object to the dog being in the house. It was clear that Buddy was used to being inside and accepting handouts whenever anything was eaten.

Bo Chapman wasn't home yet with her order when Steffi began to think about supper. Vic was puttering around with the out-of-order washing machine, and there was no indication of when he'd be ready to eat. Concern for her own stomach made Steffi start rechecking supplies.

There wasn't much on hand. She finally got a package of frozen hamburger out of the top of the refrigerator, located a couple of cans of tomato sauce, and some spaghetti. The herbs and seasonings in the cupboard looked pretty old, so they probably wouldn't be as good as those Daddy would have had, but maybe better than nothing.

She was used to defrosting with a microwave, but decided maybe if she put the meat in a frying pan, over low heat, she could defrost it a little at a time. Once, before she got the heat set right, she scorched it slightly. Buddy took care of that, and the rest of it came out fairly well.

She wasn't sure she remembered what her father had seasoned the sauce with, but she dumped the ones she thought belonged in with the simmering meat and tomato sauce. Basil, oregano, bay leaf, garlic. It would have been better with fresh stuff, especially the garlic, but there wasn't any. She wondered what Vic would have eaten if he'd been there alone.

There wasn't time to let the sauce simmer half a day, but when she tasted it, Steffi thought it was pretty good, considering. She opened a can of peas to go with the spaghetti and set the table.

When the food was ready to eat, she debated going back to tell her grandfather. He hadn't been mean to her, exactly, but he certainly hadn't made her feel welcome, either. He mostly spoke to her only when she asked him something. Maybe he'd lived alone for so long he'd gotten out of the habit of talking except to the occasional customer.

Vic came in just about the time she'd made up her

mind to go looking for him. Steffi tried to sound cheerful.

"Did you fix the washer?"

He seemed almost surprised to find her in the kitchen. "Needs a new part. I'll have to order it."

"I hope you like spaghetti," she offered nervously. "It was all I could find to make."

He washed at the kitchen sink and dried his hands before coming to the table. "Don't usually bother with cooking much," he said.

She couldn't tell if that meant he was glad she had cooked, or that it hadn't been necessary. This time, after she'd taken the chair opposite him, Steffi waited for him to say grace before they ate.

The spaghetti wasn't nearly as good as what Daddy had made, but it was edible. Maybe a little too much oregano. She knew it was easy to overuse seasonings, but how did you figure out how much?

"I don't suppose you have a cookbook," she ventured, halfway through the meal.

Vic looked up as if he'd forgotten she was there. "Must be, somewhere. Ma used to cook out of a book sometimes."

"Is it okay if I look for it?"

He shrugged, and helped himself to another serving of both the pasta and the peas. It couldn't be too bad, then, Steffi thought.

He was watching the news when a boy in his midteens came to the open doorway. "Need some bread, Vic. I can get it myself if you don't want to interrupt the news."

Vic glanced toward Steffi. "The girl'll get it for you. Price is marked on it."

"No problem, Vic, I can get it," the boy said.

Vic met Steffi's gaze in a clear command. "It's on the rack there, right in front of the counter."

Steffi moved obediently to wait on the boy. She'd never used a cash register, but it looked easy enough. She took his money, gave him change, and went back to the living room.

Vic didn't take his eyes off the black-and-white images of a fire in Chicago when he said, "Don't trust that Taylor kid. He's got sticky fingers. Never let him wait on himself."

Sticky fingers? Meaning he was a thief, given the opportunity?

Chester Taylor's boy, then. Burt. Dark hair, tall like his dad, clothes looking dirty enough to have been worn while working in a gas station. Steffi filed the information away in her mind.

She had no interest in watching the rest of the news with her grandfather. She went into the kitchen and searched through drawers and cupboards, looking for cookbooks. There were none. Maybe in the boxes still stored in her room?

Or maybe in the boxes they'd already carried out to the shed. Steffi snorted delicately. No way was she going to open up all the stuff they'd already stored. She'd try the cartons in the house.

The first box she opened, sitting cross-legged on the floor, was full of pictures. And although she'd never seen the one on top, of a little boy, it was familiar. It took her a moment to realize it reminded her of her own pictures when she was six or seven years old.

Daddy?

She'd never seen any pictures of him except on the

CAMAS PUBLIC LIBRARY

screen, and then he was always made up to look like the star of the film, and shot from the back or a distance so nobody could tell the difference. The audience was supposed to think the star was doing his own stunts.

She stared at the photo. A smiling, happy little boy.

He'd seldom talked about his childhood. She only knew that he had left home at an early age, and never returned. That his mother—Steffi's grandmother, Vic's wife—had died a long time ago. That Larry had never exchanged letters with his father.

Eagerly Steffi began to lift the photographs and snapshots out of the carton and spread them around her on the floor.

And her father's past came to life so vividly that for a time she forgot he was gone, no longer a part of her own future.

Of course not all the photos were of her father. It didn't take long to figure out that some of them—of a pleasant-looking young woman, and then of a middle-aged one—were her grandmother. Her name had been Margaret, according to the words written on the back of a few of the snapshots. Steffi had never known her grandmother's name was Margaret. It made her more real, and Steffi felt close to her at once. She wished she *had* known her.

Vic was in some of the photos, too. Far fewer than there were of her dad and his mother, but enough so she was sure they were all part of the same family. One, growing rather faded, was clearly a wedding picture, with Margaret smiling shyly and Vic looking proud.

Vic, as a young man, had looked remarkably like his

son. Steffi's breath caught in her throat, and she struggled with the wave of grief that swept over her.

After a time it dawned on Steffi that there were no cookbooks, and she put the pictures back into the box. With the exception of one, the studio portrait of a little boy. He was smiling into the camera in a way that made her heart ache, because she'd never known him that way, and she never would.

She would keep that picture out, to look at from time to time.

A sound in the doorway behind her made Steffi turn to see her grandfather.

"I . . . there were no cookbooks in here. Only photographs," she said, feeling guilty as if she'd been caught snooping.

"Try one of the boxes in the corner," Vic said. "I think I packed all the books in small boxes so they'd be easier to move."

She had instinctively hidden the photograph she'd saved out, holding it against her chest. Now she lowered it and asked him, point-blank. "Why did you hate my dad?"

For a moment she thought he wouldn't answer. His face flushed deep red under the tan, then faded out. "I never hated him," he said finally.

"But you didn't like him." *And he didn't like you,* she wanted to add. "Why? What did he do? Or what did *you* do?"

Vic's words, when they came, were heavy. "He would never listen to me. Always talked back. Argued. Fought."

Fought physically? Steffi wondered. Or only verbally? Daddy was always good with words.

Just when she thought that was all Vic was going to say on the subject, he went on. "Never could tell that boy anything. All he could think of was being in the movies. Far as I know, he never did get a decent job, just all that fooling around with cars and horses and getting his eyebrows singed off messing with explosives."

"He was a stuntman," Steffi said, just to make sure he knew.

"Never did get a decent job," Vic repeated tiredly.

"It was a good job. It paid really well," Steffi countered.

"It killed him," Vic said flatly.

"That was a freak accident. Accidents happen to everybody. Being a stuntman was his dream, and he was a good one. One of the best." Her eyes began to sting.

"Wouldn't stay in school. He was smart with book learning, he could've done anything—be a teacher, or a doctor, or a lawyer. He wouldn't have had to be stuck in a run-down trailer park like his old man. He could even have helped his ma, got her nice things, if she'd lived. He was a doggone fool," Vic stated, and turned away, finished with the topic.

Steffi cried herself to sleep that night, with Buddy's cold nose nudging her hand in canine sympathy.

She would probably have cried a lot harder if it hadn't been for Buddy.

6

Sometime during the following day, Vic must have taken away the carton of photographs. When Steffi looked for it during the evening, with the idea of removing another of the pictures, the box was no longer there.

Her first reaction was anger. If he didn't want to look at the pictures, fine. But why keep them away from her? It struck her as mean-spirited of Vic to prevent her from having that small bit of contact with family members who were no longer living.

Her second reaction was pain. It hurt to be treated as if she had never been a part of her father's family. It hurt that Vic hadn't so much as mentioned that it might be distressing to him to see those old photos, if that was why he'd taken them away. She wouldn't have displayed either the one of her father or her grandmother where he could see it.

She checked, beneath her underwear in the dresser drawer, to make sure the picture of Daddy as a boy was still there. At least he hadn't taken that one away, too.

Vic made no mention of the pictures, and Steffi couldn't bring herself to ask. He'd already made it clear he didn't care for having her there, and the thought of being further rebuffed made her throat feel tight and achy.

Bo Chapman delivered her groceries that evening, apologizing for the fact that he hadn't been able to get them sooner. "Had a crisis yesterday, one of my clerks got a finger cut off in a waxing machine. I had to get him and the finger over to the county hospital and have it sewed back on. I forgot all about your groceries."

Steffi felt her jaw sagging. "How terrible. Will he be all right?"

"They think he'll have at least limited use of the finger. He was trying to repair the waxer, and some idiot turned the power on while he was touching the belt."

Bo lowered the box onto the kitchen counter. "Some of the things on your list aren't stuff we usually stock. Like the avocados. Not too many people around here eat them, but I asked the produce man, and he had just a few. You've lived in California, right? I guess tastes are a little more exotic out there than here in backwoods Michigan. No pita bread, either. They don't make it in the local bakery. I did get some flour tortillas. You know how to fix them?"

"All kinds of ways," Steffi assured him, amazed that he wasn't familiar with what had been a staple item back home.

Steffi surveyed the wonders of fresh fruit and vegetables and nonfrozen meats. "It's a whole lot better than corned beef hash and canned peas. Thanks a lot."

"Any time. Just give me your lists," Mr. Chapman said.

It had already become obvious to Steffi that if they were going to eat anything other than stuff out of cans, she'd have to fix it. She did manage to find a few cookbooks in one of the other boxes in her bedroom, but they were very old and didn't seem to have recipes for many of the dishes she had helped her dad to make. So she experimented a little, trying to remember what her father had done.

When Vic sat down at the table and looked at chicken enchiladas in cheese sauce with black olives dotting the surface, his expression froze.

"What is it?" he asked.

"Enchiladas. I couldn't get any green chiles, so they won't have quite as much flavor, but I tasted one of them. They're pretty good."

Looking as if they might poison him, Vic tried a bite. It hadn't even occurred to her that he might not like her favorite foods if someone cooked them for him.

It was impossible to tell by his face what he thought of the enchiladas, and he didn't comment on them. He did, however, go back for a second helping.

And that, Steffi supposed, was as much of a compliment as she was going to get.

She'd made a salad, too. Her mother, always trying to stay slim for possible movie roles, had eaten lots of salads, and Steffi had learned to like them and to make interesting ones. This first one was quite simple: lettuce, tomato, green onions, and a garnish of grated cheese and sunflower seeds.

Vic had inspected that before tasting, also. "What are those things? Look like birdseed."

She told him. "They're good. Crunchy."

Again, Vic finished his meal off without a word. Well, at least he hadn't dumped the meal in the garbage and made himself a peanut butter sandwich instead.

Over the next few days she tried beef stew with dumplings, Cajun fried chicken, pork chops baked with a sage dressing, and homemade pizza. Vic inspected each offering silently, tasted gingerly, then cleaned his plate. All without any comment.

Even when she experimented, rather successfully Steffi thought, with a canned cherry pie filling over package mix cheesecake, her grandfather never said a grateful word.

"I give up," she told Casey in disgust. "No wonder my father didn't get along with him. There's no way to please him."

"So go back to canned hash and peas," Casey suggested, grinning.

"No. I'll cook for myself, stuff I like. And I won't expect any praise for it, no matter how good it is, so I won't be disappointed."

"Way to go," Casey approved.

Buddy lived up to his name, following Steffi everywhere. He slept beside her bed, where she could reach over and drop a hand onto his big head. He laid on the edge of the pool while she worked in its depths, scouring off the grime of the past winter. He sat by her feet when she ate, although under her grandfather's scrutiny she didn't dare sneak him tidbits. That was reserved for the times when she and the dog were alone. When she walked through the woods or out to the mailbox, Buddy tagged along.

There was a postcard from her mother at the end of her first week in Michigan. A glowing picture of red rocks against an impossibly blue sky, and a brief note. *All's well so far. The director is exacting, but fair. It's hot. How are you getting along with Grampa? Love, Mom.*

Grampa. Hah! Steffi snorted, and stuck the card in the top drawer of her dresser.

It took a full week to clean out the pool so that it could be refilled. Everybody in the campground came around and offered encouragement or advice, but nobody else helped with the work. Steffi and Casey did it all, with Buddy's supervision.

The day they began to refill it was cause for celebration. It filled very slowly, to Steffi's eyes. She could hardly tell that the water was getting deeper unless she stayed away for several hours at a time.

Late in the afternoon she was in the store, selling bread and milk to Mrs. Montoni while Vic pumped propane for Kurt Vail. Mr. Vail waited to pay for his gas and watched Steffi ring up the cash register.

"The pool ready to go?" he asked.

"As soon as Casey gets the chemicals adjusted right," Steffi said, handing over change to Mrs. Montoni.

"It's got an automatic filter. Shouldn't be too bad to keep in good shape, especially if you cover it with that sheet of plastic at night to keep dirt out of it. You kids did a great job," Mr. Vail said. "You know, we ought to have a party when it's ready to swim in. The whole camp."

"That's a great idea," Mrs. Montoni said. "Why don't we have a picnic tomorrow evening, everybody together, and then try out the pool?"

"I'll bring hot dogs," Mr. Vail offered. "I'll get enough for everybody, and we'll cook them on the grill."

And so it was arranged, with all the others notified. To Steffi's surprise, even Helen Risku agreed to participate. With the food, she made clear, not with the swimming.

"Did you decide Mr. Vail was harmless?" Steffi couldn't help asking.

"Not exactly," Helen said. "But if he's going to stay on, I can't be a hermit. I can't even go out for some fresh air, or to walk Barkley, without him seeing me. After all, he's parked right next door."

"I'm glad you're coming to the party, then," Steffi told her, bending over to pet Barkley.

"He asks a lot of questions," Helen said.

"Yes. I've noticed."

"If he asks you about me, pretend you don't know anything," Helen urged, quite serious.

"I really don't know anything," Steffi reminded her.

"Not where I'm from or how old I am, or anything."

"Right," Steffi agreed. And then later, to Casey, "I can't imagine what she thinks I'd tell a stranger that would put her in any kind of danger."

She expected Casey to laugh it off, but he was thoughtful. "She probably has secrets, same as everybody else. Whatever hers are, she wants them to stay secret."

Teasing, Steffi said, "Do you have secrets, too, Casey?"

"Sure. Why else would we be living in a crummy

little trailer in a dump like this?" He grinned. "Dad and I are hiding out from the cops. We robbed a bank in Detroit."

"Okay," Steffi said agreeably. "While the water keeps running, I'm going to get out last year's swimsuit and see if it still fits. See you later."

She had grown, so the suit seemed skimpy, but it was in two pieces and since she hadn't gotten any bigger around, just taller, it would do.

Later on, seeing Chester Taylor walk past the front of the building, Steffi had an uncomfortable thought.

Casey had laughed about it, but somehow she didn't think the laughter had reached his eyes, the way it usually did. Was he joking about the truth? Was there really some grim reason why he and his dad were here at Hidden Valley?

Her grandfather's campground would be a good place to hide out, for anyone who didn't want to attract attention to himself. Someone like Chester Taylor, who struck her as a man she'd choose to play a thug in a gangster movie. And his son Burt, who was perhaps a thief.

Did Helen Risku really have some reason to hide? Not from paranoia, but because there actually was some risk to being spotted? Who on earth would endanger an old lady like Helen? *She* certainly wasn't a fugitive. But maybe the Chapmans could be, or even Kurt Vail, who had come to fish for a day or two and was still here, nosing into the lives of his fellow campers in such a friendly way that so far nobody had told him to mind his own business.

Up to now Steffi hadn't even had a glimpse of the

man who lived in the old motorhome, way at the far end of camp. She knew his name was Oliver Mandell, because Casey had said so, but he never seemed to come out of his coach. The occupant of the trailer next to him had remained invisible, too.

Were there, as Casey had suggested, secrets all these people kept to themselves? This was a good place for it. As faded as the sign was out on the main road, it was a miracle anyone ever spotted it and came in to stay at the campground. Most everyone was a permanent resident, it seemed. There were few overnighters.

Even Vic, who owned the place but didn't seem interested in keeping things up enough to attract tourists, had his secrets, Steffi thought. Was it enough, because your son had gone into work you thought was foolish, to break all contact with him? Not even to react when you heard the son had died?

Maybe there'd been a clue she hadn't caught in that box of photographs. She wondered where Vic had put it.

At last the pool was filled. It was almost dark when Casey came to tell her he'd turned off the inflow and put in the chemicals.

"Should we try it out, do you think?" he asked.

"Everybody's expecting to do that when we have the party tomorrow night. Will they think we cheated if we go in now?"

Casey sighed. "Yeah. Probably. Okay, we'll wait until we have the party. But we swim *before* the hot dogs, right?"

Steffi nodded. When she went inside, she told Vic the pool was ready to use. He didn't even look up from the paper, only grunted to acknowledge that he'd heard her.

Even if he had had a genuine reason for hating his

son, he had none for disliking *her,* Steffi thought angrily as she went on through the room to her own cramped little cubicle. She hadn't done anything to make him angry.

Except coming here, uninvited. The thought came to her, unbidden, unwelcome.

She threw herself down across the bed and thought about what her mother was doing on location in New Mexico. It would be wonderful to be there, too. How long would it be before that shoot was finished so they could both go home to California?

Buddy crept silently up to lick the hand that dangled over the edge of the bed.

She spoke to him in a voice too low to carry to the living room. "I'll be glad to leave, Buddy. But I'll miss you. I never could have a dog. We didn't stay home enough, we always went wherever the movies were being made. It was hard to make friends, too, when I didn't even go to school all the time. Mom was a pretty good home-school teacher, but I missed having other kids around. A dog would have helped. Vic will be glad when I leave, but you'll miss me, won't you?"

Buddy's tail swished back and forth.

"Maybe before I go I'll put sandburs in his bed," she thought aloud. "Or leave his refrigerator doors open, so the food will defrost and spoil. I'd steal *you* if they'd take you on the bus. You wouldn't fit in my suitcase."

Buddy licked up her arm and caught her chin before she could jerk it out of the way.

"I'm homesick, Buddy," she whispered, wrapping an arm around his neck. "If it weren't for you and Casey, I'd really hate it here, even with a swimming pool."

For a while, until she fell asleep without ever putting on her pajamas, she lay there and thought about the good times she'd had with Dad and Mom, back when she was still part of a real family. She'd always wanted a brother or a sister, but Mom had said that wouldn't be practical, not with parents who couldn't stay in one place. Steffi didn't care what was practical, she just wanted a family like other kids had. But even with only the three of them, they'd had a lot of fun. At least until Daddy died. Nothing had been fun since then.

When she woke up later, well into the night, she was cold on one side and warm on the other. Steffi sat halfway up to figure it out and realized that Buddy was curled beside her, keeping her warm.

Half smiling, she managed to get a blanket up and over both of them. Good old Buddy, she thought. He was *almost* as good as a family.

The pool party was a huge success. Everyone in the campground came, bringing buns for the hot dogs, chips, baked beans, lemonade, and a platter of raw vegetables and dips. The elderly couple who lived behind the Montonis, Carrie and Herbert Johnson, brought their ice-cream freezer to provide dessert.

It was fun to meet the residents of the Hidden Valley RV Park that she hadn't seen before. Some of them, like the Parkers, worked and were gone all day. The old bachelors, Oliver Mandell and his neighbor, Elwood Grisham, usually kept to themselves. And lastly there was Mrs. Evans. She was a round, jolly, middle-aged woman who had bad knees, as she explained to Steffi, so she wasn't able to get out and walk much, but she always enjoyed company. Casey's dad actually drove her up to the pool-side area so she wouldn't have to walk that far. People had brought lawn chairs, and there were a couple of picnic tables provided by the campground, where they set out the food.

"Where's Vic?" Bo Chapman asked Steffi, depositing an ice chest of canned pop beside her. "Isn't he joining us?"

"I don't know," Steffi said. "I heard Mrs. Montoni telling him about it, so he knows everybody's invited. I don't think he's very social."

"We better let him know when we're ready to eat, anyway," Bo decided. "What had you kids decided? Swim first, then have supper?"

"Yeah," Casey said. "Swim while it's still hot."

It *was* hot, but they hadn't given the water in the pool time to warm up. When Steffi plunged in, in a tie with Casey, she felt as if she'd gone into ice water that paralyzed her respiratory system. She came to the surface, gasping.

A few feet away Casey surfaced, too, laughing. "Wow! Is this refreshing or what?"

Most of the adults didn't even dip a toe in. Mr. and Mrs. Montoni came in with their kids, very briefly, then retreated to sit on the edge and watch until Danny and Jenny turned blue. The little one, Gus, had wanted out almost immediately. The family reminded Steffi of the fun she and Daddy and Mom used to have.

Just before everyone was ready to start broiling the hot dogs, the Taylors showed up. Burt shucked off jeans and a plaid shirt to reveal a pair of loud, red-flowered trunks, and dove in off the diving board; he went all the way to the bottom on the deep end, came up blowing air and swiping back his rather longish hair, and immediately climbed out to grab for his shirt.

"Cold, huh?" his father said, obviously having no intention of testing the temperature.

"Yeah," Burt agreed. "I'm gonna cover up my goose pimples. Let this thing warm up a little and it'll be great."

Steffi, sitting on the sidelines by this time, observed that goose pimples weren't the only thing Burt covered up. She leaned over to whisper to Casey.

"Did you notice the bruises?"

"On his back and his shoulder," Casey confirmed. "Looks like his dad's been knocking him around again."

Steffi's eyes were wide. "Does he do that often?"

"Three or four times that I know of, in the three months I've been here," Casey confirmed.

"You'd think somebody—Burt himself—would notify the authorities if his dad's abusing him."

"Somebody did, once at least," Casey told her in a low voice. "Chester convinced the guy who came that the kid asked for it, for stealing. They told him he couldn't beat on him even if he did steal, and he said he wouldn't hit him anymore."

"But he does." Steffi soberly considered what it would be like to have an abusive father. And that made her wonder if Vic had mistreated *her* father, if that was the reason Larry had left home at such an early age. It was a disturbing idea.

Kurt Vail was presiding over the three grills that had been hauled into the picnic area. The aroma of sizzling hot dogs drifted to where Steffi sat, and she got up. "It smells like they're almost ready." Vic wasn't there but maybe he didn't like hot dogs. Or was it that he didn't like parties?

Bo Chapman came back after looking for Vic, shaking his head. "Vic's not feeling sociable today," he reported.

Steffi didn't think he ever felt sociable. But the aroma of roasting wieners made her forget about her grandfather.

The Montoni kids were the first to be served, because they were the youngest, and then the others took paper plates and lined up. Steffi, plate so heavily loaded it threatened to fold up unless she kept a hand under it, sat down next to Helen Risku. "Looks good, doesn't it? I told Mr. Vail I wanted one almost burned. I like them that way."

Helen shot a glance at Mr. Vail as he turned over the meat on the grill and added more to replace what had already been served. "He asked me where I was from," she muttered under her breath.

"What did you tell him?" Steffi asked. She couldn't see what difference it made.

"I told him I'd been here so long I hardly remembered."

Casey, easing onto the bench on the other side of the table, leaned forward to offer advice. "If it bothers you, why didn't you just say it was none of his business?"

"He's a detective," Helen said unexpectedly. "I know he is."

A detective? Steffi looked at Casey, anticipating that he would find this as unlikely as she did, especially that a detective would be investigating a lady who was nearly ninety years old.

For just a few seconds, though, Steffi was confounded by the expression on Casey's face.

He looked, in that unguarded moment, as if he were taking Helen's opinion very seriously indeed, and as if it had some personal significance. Then he took a bite of his baked beans and said, "He's probably just a guy on vacation."

The expression was gone. Instinctively, Steffi glanced toward Casey's father, who was also close enough to have overheard Helen's comment.

And on Bo's face, too, was . . . what? A wariness, a trace of apprehension? Then he reached for the mustard and slathered it lavishly on his hot dog, leaving Steffi to wonder if she'd imagined the entire thing.

Chester Taylor had just sat down on one of the benches on the far side of the table from Steffi. His weight made the wooden planks creak. Otherwise she probably wouldn't have noticed that he, too, seemed to react to Helen's remark a few seconds earlier when he'd been leaning past her to reach the catsup bottle.

"Detective?" he echoed. "You mean the guy's a cop?"

"No," Helen said flatly. "A private detective, of course."

Chester had forgotten that he was squeezing the bottle over his hot dog. Catsup spouted out over his hand and ran down his arm, so that he suddenly cursed and grabbed for a handful of napkins. By that time, the mess was too big for paper napkins, and he got up and headed for a nearby hose connection to wash himself off.

Helen looked after him with distaste. "Such a vulgar man," she said.

Steffi, transfixed by the reactions of the others to

what she had assumed was an insignificant remark from a confused old woman, had forgotten to eat.

"How can you tell by looking at him," she asked quietly, staring not at Chester Taylor but at the man turning hot dogs on the grill, "that he's a detective?"

"It isn't just looking at him, dear, though he does have the look of a flat foot, doesn't he?" The expression, coming from this rather ancient lady, would have made Steffi laugh, except that no one else at their table was amused by it. "He's done nothing but ask questions since he got here. He says he's staying for the fishing, but how much time has he actually spent out in his boat? Why hasn't he caught any fish? Elwood and Oliver both catch at least a few when they go out."

Steffi waited for one of the Chapmans to dispute the evidence that Kurt Vail was a detective, private or otherwise, but they didn't. They just changed the subject and started passing around the bowl of potato salad Helen had brought.

Steffi couldn't put it out of her mind throughout the evening, which lasted until it began to get dark and the mosquitoes came out. When the party finally broke up and the debris was cleared away, she and Casey and Bo rolled the dark plastic sheet over the pool.

"Leave it on at least until noon," Bo advised, "and solar power will help heat the water."

He sounded subdued, or was he only tired? Steffi couldn't tell.

Vic was still reading the paper when Steffi came in.

She hesitated for a moment, then blurted, "Mrs. Risku thinks that Kurt Vail is a private detective."

Vic looked up at her. "Private detectives take vacations and like to fish, same as anybody else," he said.

"Is he, then? Do you know?"

"I don't ask people what they do for a living. Only their home addresses and their license numbers."

So the matter was unresolved, but Steffi couldn't help thinking about it after she'd gone to bed and Buddy had surreptitiously hoisted himself up to rest his head on her feet.

Clearly Helen believed what she'd said, and it bothered her in a personal way. And from what Steffi had observed, both the Chapmans and the Taylors had taken Helen seriously, maybe also for their own personal reasons.

A person would have to be demented, Steffi thought, to believe that people in three different families, in this little campground, would be anxious about the possibility of a detective in their midst. Yet, what else could she think?

Chester Taylor had immediately assumed "detective" meant "cop," and maybe that was understandable if his son had been in trouble with the law in the past. Yet even if Burt had stolen something, it would be a uniformed police officer who came after him, wouldn't it? She knew Helen was peculiar, but why would it matter to Casey and Bo if Vail was a law officer?

After lifting the plastic tarp in midmorning, Casey decided the water in the pool needed to warm up some more. "You want to go fishing?" he asked Steffi. "It's kind of late, most people go early in the morning, but we might catch a few."

"Can we fish from the shore?" Steffi asked, eager to do anything besides sit around reading the decrepit old

Westerns and detective stories that filled Vic's bookshelves.

"No, not very well. But Oliver and Elwood aren't out today; they'd probably let us use their boat."

Steffi trotted along with Casey to ask. Both Oliver Mandell and Elwood Grisham lived frugally on small pensions. Both of them, according to Casey, pretty much kept to themselves.

"You must have been doing some detective work of your own," Steffi suggested, "as much as you've found out in only three months."

Casey grinned. "I learned most of what I know from listening to Helen. She's been here long enough to know everything about everybody. Oliver and Elwood were here before she came, I guess. Oliver's a retired English teacher, and Elwood used to manage a building supply company in St. Ignace."

Steffi had been introduced to both men at the picnic, but hadn't really talked to either of them. She found Elwood's trailer and Oliver's dilapidated motorhome interesting when they were invited into each of them.

Oliver was a rather pudgy, soft-looking man, with a fringe of graying hair just above his ears, and a shiny bald pate. He was soft-spoken, too, and quite cordial. His motorhome was filled with books. They covered every flat surface. He turned down the music (a Chopin polonaise, which Steffi recognized because it had been the theme song of a movie her dad had worked on) and started to clear off chairs for them to sit in.

"No, we can't stay," Casey stopped him. "We just wanted to know if there was a chance we could borrow your boat for a couple of hours. Until the pool warms up a little more."

"Oh. Well, I've no intention of using it. But it's half Elwood's boat, so you better ask him, too. Sometimes he takes it out by himself, you know."

"Okay. Thanks, Oliver." Casey turned to leave, then paused. "What did you think of that new guy, Kurt Vail? Helen thinks he's a private detective."

Oliver's eyebrows went up. "Oh? Well, could be. He asks enough questions, doesn't he? On the other hand, Helen's a bit batty sometimes, you know? Harmless, of course, but doesn't always seem to have both oars in the water."

They went next door to Elwood's trailer. Elwood invited them in, a hunched, skinny man with a full head of gray hair that resembled a Brillo pad. His living quarters were crowded, too, but not with books, although there were a few of them around. Elwood's hobby was building models.

When Steffi exclaimed over an exquisite little castle, constructed entirely of toothpicks and balsa wood, Elwood beamed. "That's a nice one, isn't it? Took me three months, last winter, when we were snowed in most of the time. Do you like ships? That one over there is the U.S.S. *Constitution.* I saw the real one once, fascinating. It's anchored in Boston Harbor. You ever been to Boston?"

They both had to admit they had not.

"Ever get a chance, go. Fascinating, Boston. It's like walking through history. What can I do for you young folks this morning?"

"We wanted to know if we could borrow your boat for a few hours. Oliver said he didn't care if you didn't."

"Oh, sure. We may go out early tomorrow, but not today. Go ahead and take it."

"Thanks. We appreciate it." Again Casey hesitated. "Nice picnic last night, wasn't it?"

Elwood bobbed his steel-wool—like hair. "Very nice."

"Did you meet everybody? Steffi, here, and the new guy, Kurt Vail?"

"Yes, yes," Elwood said.

"Helen thinks Mr. Vail is a detective."

"Does she, now? Well, I shouldn't wonder if Helen's right. At times she can be quite astute. She knew when I had a bleeding ulcer, you know. Took one look at me and said I was the wrong color, suggested I see a doctor at once. Internal bleeding, she said. She probably saved my life. All right now, though."

So they had two opinions about Helen. And neither man had actually rejected the idea that the newest resident of the campground was a detective.

Casey had been quite casual with his questions, Steffi thought as she padded behind him along the path to the lake a few minutes later. But it seemed he, too, was concerned about a detective, private or police, in their midst.

She couldn't quite bring herself to ask him why—he might, as he'd suggested to Helen, tell her it was none of her business. Yet the question wouldn't leave her.

8

Casey caught two small fish, and Steffi caught one. It was kind of fun, bringing the gleaming, twisting fish up through the clear water. She had no particular desire to handle it, though. "If you put it with yours, there's maybe enough to feed two people," she said as Casey dropped it into the bucket they'd brought along.

"Okay. You and Vic eat these, and Dad and I will take the next batch." Casey reached for the oars. "Let's see if the pool has warmed up yet."

It hadn't, of course. Casey had to make the rounds of the camp, collecting plastic bags of trash to haul up to the big Dumpster, and Steffi helped him with that before she went in the house.

She reported their catch to her grandfather, but Vic

only muttered an acknowledgment. Disgruntled, she wondered what it would take to please him.

Chester Taylor's pickup was parked at the foot of the steps, but there was no sign of the man. Steffi looked around, a little uneasy, because she knew Vic wouldn't want him to go into the store when no one was there. She hesitated, looking into the cab at a collection of jackets, tools, and candy wrappers on the seat, then jumped when the man's voice boomed behind her.

"What are you snooping around for?" he demanded.

She stared at him. "I wasn't snooping. I just wondered if you needed something from the store."

"If I want something, I'll say so. Don't go messing around my truck," Chester warned her.

Indignation bubbled inside her, but Steffi had no desire to tangle with the man. She didn't think he'd dare hit anybody else's kid, but who knew? He obviously had a nasty temper.

She didn't answer him, but went down the steps and around the truck. She had barely reached the drive when the motor roared behind her, and Chester floored it, going past her. She didn't think he could have missed brushing against her by more than a few inches. Her heart pounded as she stared after the truck.

Steffi made a note to stay as far away from the Taylors as she could. But Vic was a bigger problem, and there was no way she could stay away from *him.*

She walked out to the mailbox, with Buddy tagging along. There was a letter from her mother. Steffi read it perched on the front steps. Mom wrote about how the shoot was going, and mentioned that the director's assistant, Candy, had ruptured her appendix and was in the

hospital in Albuquerque, where they'd taken her by heli-copter. The director, whose name was Ron, had asked Audri to fill in on Candy's job, and it had been sort of interesting. They were going to move in a few days, so she couldn't provide an address for Steffi to write back, but she hoped all was going well.

And what if it wasn't? What if *I* had a ruptured appendix, she thought grumpily, and had to go into the hospital? How would you even know? If I was really sick, I couldn't call Majestic Films to hunt you down.

When she had a child of her own, Steffi decided, she wouldn't run all over the country making movies. Kids needed someone around they could depend on. Like Mrs. Montoni, who was always taking her kids for walks, or reading to them, or playing games on the picnic table.

When Vic came over to the store to wait on Oliver, Steffi handed him the rest of the mail. He threw it down carelessly on the counter while he got Oliver's carton of milk, and several of the letters slid over the edge. One of them wedged between the counter and the end of the case where Vic kept the frozen items.

Steffi saw it go and got the edge of the letter between her fingernails to pull it out. Then she saw that there was another letter in there, too, but she couldn't reach it.

She looked around for something thin enough to go into the crack. Failing to find anything at hand, she brought a boning knife from the kitchen and fished the other letter out.

She recognized the handwriting. It was the letter her mother had written telling Vic that unless she heard from him to the contrary, she was putting Steffi on a bus to come here.

She stared at it. No wonder he'd been surprised when she turned up.

She laid the letter beside the cash register, and started to leave the store. Before she reached the hall, though, Vic spoke.

"Girl, you want to deliver this to Mrs. Evans? She don't get much mail, and she can't walk this far very well, so I usually take it over to her. Might as well take this one to Helen Risku, too, long as you'll be going right next door to her."

Girl. For a moment the impact of that almost kept Steffi from registering the rest of it. He was her grandfather, but so far he'd never said her name. Nor indicated in any way, other than cleaning his plate even when she fixed food he'd never tried before, that he was paying any attention to her.

Well, to be fair, he had let her order the groceries she wanted. Still, it hurt that he refused to use her name.

She accepted the letters he handed over, and walked through the park, Buddy accompanying her at a leisurely pace.

If she got stuck here all summer, would he ever say her name? Did he even remember what it was?

He was a disagreeable old man, so why did it matter? Why did it make her eyes burn, as if she were going to cry?

Mrs. Evans welcomed her with a smile. "Oh, a letter from my daughter in Houston. Thank you, dear, how thoughtful of you to bring it over. Come on in a minute, can you? I've just baked some chocolate-chip cookies. Sit down, right there on the couch."

The little trailer was cozy and pleasant for all its lack of space. There was a mound of crocheting in variegated

pinks and greens, a magazine open on the kitchen table, little ceramic animals on tiny shelves and windowsills. Steffi ate two cookies and accepted a paper plateful to carry back home with her. But Mrs. Evans was eager for company, for someone to talk to. It would have been cruel not to visit for a few minutes.

"Nice party last night, wasn't it? We should do that more often," Mrs. Evans said.

"No reason why we can't, I guess," Steffi asserted. She made polite responses to questions about her family and how they'd lived in Hollywood. The fact that her father had been a stuntman and that her mother was an actress seemed very glamorous to Mrs. Evans. Obviously she didn't share Vic's opinion that it was all foolishness and that they should have given it up for "real" jobs.

Steffi finally decided it was time to move on. She was glad Mrs. Evans had put plastic wrap over the plate of cookies, since she still had to stop at Helen's place and carry them past Barkley. "Thank you for the cookies, they're delicious." They'd had mostly store-bought cookies when Daddy was alive, when they were still a family. He'd never been into baking much.

Helen answered the door with enthusiasm to equal her neighbor's. For Steffi's company, not for the mail. She glanced at her letter and dropped it on her minuscule table. "From the library. I've forgotten to return one of my books."

The ugly little dog was leaping around Steffi's feet in greeting. "Hi, Barkley," Steffi said, holding the cookies out of his reach.

"Shhh!" Helen said quickly. "Not so loud, dear! He'll hear you!"

"Who?" Steffi asked blankly, looking over her shoulder. There was Kurt Vail, resting in a lawn chair not more than twenty feet away. "Him, you mean?"

"Yes. Don't say Barkley's name where he can hear you." She was whispering. "He's the reason I didn't let Barkley come to the party with me, you know. He mustn't hear Barkley's name."

"Why not?" Steffi asked, wondering who was right, Elwood, who thought Helen was astute, or Oliver, who thought she was batty.

"If he recognizes the dog's name, then he'll know it's me," Helen told her. "I don't use my real first name here, you know. It's really Dorothy. Helen's a name I just made up. I used to have a friend named Helen when I was in sixth grade. I couldn't bear to give up my darling Frankie's name, though. Sixty-four years we were married. And Risku isn't all that uncommon a name around here. Lots of Finnish people." She peered through the screen at Kurt Vail. "So he may not know who I am if you don't mention the dog's name."

Steffi felt a bit confused, making her way back out the door. But she liked Helen. Or Dorothy. Or whatever her name was. She didn't understand what Barkley's name had to do with anything, though.

Kurt Vail looked up from the book he was reading. "Hello, there. You tried out that pool yet today?"

"It's still like ice," Steffi said, not pausing to visit. "We went out on the lake instead."

"Catch anything?"

"One little fish," Steffi said, and kept on walking away from him.

Mr. Montoni was just pulling away from the storage

shed when she reached him. He had his pickup loaded with all kinds of junk.

"Hi, Steffi. I picked up the stuff Vic said to take out of the shed to the dump. So you can move the rest of the boxes out of your room."

"Okay." Steffi hesitated, noticing some of the items in the truck. "Is that paint you're throwing away?"

"Yeah. There were a lot of old paint cans, not enough of any one color to do anything very big, so he said I could get rid of them."

The faded welcoming sign for the campground was right alongside the truck, and she spoke impulsively. "Is there enough so I could repaint the signs? It's a wonder to me anybody notices the one out on the highway, it's so pale. And it's half hidden behind the trees until you get right up to it."

"Maybe I could trim some of the branches. You want the paint? Sure, help yourself," Mr. Montoni said.

So Steffi retrieved all the cans of paint, and went off to the shed for the paintbrushes she'd seen there when they got out the scrub brushes.

There was time, she decided, to paint at least the nearby sign before it got dark. And maybe tomorrow she'd go out to the main road and start on that sign, too. It wasn't that the campground had all that many empty spaces most of the time, but if Vic was doing this in order to earn a living, he might as well have a sign that could bring in enough customers to keep all the spaces filled.

She painted the background yellow, softened from its original bright hue by mixing it with a light cream. The lettering she did in red. She stepped back to admire the result, and wondered if Vic would approve. She hadn't thought to ask him about it beforehand, but it was such an improvement he would surely be pleased. Even if he didn't say so.

So they'd be ready when she had time to paint the other sign, she carefully cleaned out the brushes and stuck everything in a cupboard in the laundry room.

There was only one other box in the cupboard, and Steffi recognized it. Vic had put a wide tape over the flaps on the top, so she couldn't get into it to look at the pictures again without cutting the tape.

Steffi sighed. It made her feel bad that her grandfather clearly wanted to keep her out of a box that held all those pictures of her father and grandmother. Why didn't Vic want her to claim that part of her heritage?

The following morning Casey showed up early to ask if she wanted to go fishing again, since Oliver and Elwood were going to town and wouldn't be using their boat after all.

It seemed better than doing nothing, so she packed a lunch for Casey and herself, and met him while there was still a drift of fog over the lake. Mr. Vail's boat was pulled up on the shore, and Casey glanced at it.

"He doesn't seem to use the boat much, does he? Makes you wonder why he hauled it all the way from Indiana if he's not going to fish."

Buddy had followed them and wagged his tail hopefully, until Casey shrugged. "All right, get in," he invited, and the big black dog leaped eagerly into the rowboat.

It was pleasant out on the water, but Steffi soon became bored with fishing. Especially since they didn't catch anything.

She scanned the shoreline. There were scattered cabins around the lake; the owners came out for vacations or weekends. Steffi wondered if there were kids in any of the places. It was going to be a long summer if all she and Casey had to do was swim or sit in a boat waiting for fish that didn't bite.

They ate their lunches sitting in the boat on the far side of the lake from the campground. It was quiet and peaceful, and Steffi thought her dad might have liked it.

"Dad never had time to fish that I know of," she told Casey, "but he enjoyed this kind of thing. Sunshine, fresh air, calm water. He liked rough water, rapids, too, though."

Casey murmured a reply. "It's nice," he agreed.

It occurred to Steffi that Casey, too, had only one parent. "My dad died in a horrible accident," she told him. It was the first time she'd talked to another kid about it here. "Did your mom die, too?"

Casey's face went still. "No. She's still alive. She lives in Ohio. My folks have been divorced for almost two years."

"Oh. I'm sorry. Do you get to see her very often?"

"No," Casey said quietly. "You want me to row next?"

Rowing was harder than Steffi had expected, and she was glad Casey liked doing it. She sat in the back of the boat and watched the forested shore slide by, thinking about having a mother but not seeing her. Would that be even harder than losing a parent to death? She knew she'd never see Daddy again, but what if you loved a parent who was alive but too far away to visit? Did Casey miss his mother or not? She couldn't tell from the way he'd answered, and there was something about him that made her hesitant to ask.

They got back to the campground in the early afternoon. Casey suggested a swim but the pool was still icy enough so they got out after about ten minutes.

"Give it another day in the sun," Casey predicted, "and it'll be great. Dad told me to run a couple of loads of laundry, so I'll see you later."

Steffi got out the paint and the brushes and found a few old rags. Buddy happily fell into step beside her as she set out for the main road.

It wasn't a large sign, but it took her until nearly suppertime to paint it. She did the lettering with care, wanting it to look professional.

There wasn't enough of the yellow/cream mixture to do all the background on this sign, so she used the deep blue, with lettering in the lighter color, and just a touch of red to shade the words and Vic's name. Then, on impulse, she lettered in FISHING—POOL. When she'd finished and stepped back to examine it, she was pleased. The sign would be much easier to see from the road than it had been before; it ought to bring in more customers. Particularly since Mr. Montoni had already cut off a few of the cedar branches that had partially obscured it.

She was pleasantly tired by the time she reached the house. Somewhere in camp someone was barbecuing, and the aroma made her mouth water. She ran through the possibilities for supper as she entered the front door. She'd hoped they'd catch enough fish to fry. Now what?

Tacos, maybe. Would Vic like tacos? Or macaroni and cheese. Or maybe both, in case he thought tacos were too exotic. Vic thought anything anybody ate in California was exotic.

Buddy trotted ahead of her, disappearing into the far end of the hallway. A moment later, as she entered the living quarters, she heard him bark.

Steffi poked her head back into the corridor. "Buddy?" she called.

The barking intensified; the dog sounded frantic.

Probably a squirrel got inside and he's got it cornered in the laundry room, Steffi thought. She moved toward the sounds, and then stopped short in the doorway to the backyard.

There was no one in the laundry, not even Buddy. The screen door stood ajar, where the dog had forced it open, and she peered out.

Buddy barked, then whimpered, as Steffi stood riveted over him.

A tall ladder had fallen diagonally across the sidewalk, and beside it lay a limp figure in jeans and a plaid work shirt rolled up to the elbows.

"Vic?" Steffi asked uncertainly. And then, as she stepped nearer, "Grandpa?"

By that time, she was in a position to see the blood pooling around her grandfather's head, spreading out over the concrete.

9

Steffi's heart pounded so hard it almost drowned out Buddy's whining and her own voice. "Grandpa! Can you hear me?"

The old man was motionless, and panic swept over her. What were you supposed to do in a situation like this? In the city Steffi knew to call 911, but how about here, out in the backwoods?

Buddy whimpered, nudging Vic's shoulder. Steffi grasped his collar and pulled him back. "Sit, Buddy. Stay. I've got to get help."

Buddy sat back on his haunches, but continued to make that distressed sound deep in his throat.

Steffi fled through the building and collided with Casey as she emerged onto the front porch. Kurt Vail was just coming up the shallow steps and reeled backward when Steffi knocked Casey into him.

"Whoa," Mr. Vail said. "Is something wrong?"

"My grandpa—Vic needs help. He's knocked out, he didn't answer me!"

"What happened?" Casey asked. "Are you hurt? You're bleeding!"

"I . . . I must have touched it. It's his blood. Please, come help!"

Mr. Vail hurried ahead, with Steffi explaining as they went. Just as they reached the rear screen door, Buddy threw his nose up and howled.

Steffi felt the impact of that cry along every nerve. Kurt Vail was through the doorway and kneeling beside the old man, careless of the blood he was getting on the knees of his pants. He reached for one outstretched wrist and felt it.

"He's got a good strong pulse. But he's had a nasty knock on the head. Better get an ambulance out here, Casey. You have money for the phone?"

He shifted his weight to dig into a pocket for coins, which he dropped into Casey's hand.

"Nearest ambulance has to come quite a ways," Casey said, hesitating. "There's a retired doctor has a summer place in town. Maybe I should try to get him."

Mr. Vail nodded. "Okay. Here, looks like he's beginning to come around a little. Vic? Mr. Tomaschek? Can you hear me?"

Vic groaned and moved ever so slightly.

"Don't try to get up," Mr. Vail told him, resting a hand on his shoulder. "We're getting a doctor. I don't think we'd better move you until he gets here."

88

Before the doctor arrived, everybody in camp knew there had been an accident.

Elwood looked up at the eaves, and then at the ladder sprawled across the sidewalk. "He said he was going to clean out the gutters. That's what he was doing, all right. Looks like the ladder skidded out from under him."

Oliver nodded. "Right not to move him. He's had a real whack on the head."

Vic groaned, and Steffi bit hard on her lower lip. He might have been killed when his head hit the concrete.

There was a murmur behind Steffi, and she turned to see a man with gray hair and one of the loudest plaid shirts she'd ever imagined, walking toward the group carrying a leather bag.

"Hi, Doc," Elwood said, making way for him. "Thought you retired two years ago."

"I tried," the doctor said, his eyes on Vic. "People keep doing fool things to themselves, and keep calling me. Move back, please. Let's see what we have here."

"Ladder . . . went out from under me," Vic mumbled, trying to sit up.

"Take it easy, Vic. You know who I am?"

There was blood on the side of Vic's head, which had trickled into one eye. He made a swipe at it, winced, and managed to prop himself up. "Yes, I know who you are. Hank Daniels. Local quack."

Steffi's breath caught in her throat, but the doctor laughed.

"Right. Same one who delivered your son, fixed your broken foot, stitched up your face when you went through the windshield of that 1941 Ford. Anything damaged besides your head?"

"You're the doctor," Vic almost snarled. "You're supposed to tell *me*."

"Right." Dr. Daniels glanced around at the spectators. "How about two of you fellows getting him into the house where I can take a decent look at him?"

Everyone was excluded while the examination took place. Steffi waited with the others, immensely relieved that the doctor had taken charge.

She was badly shaken, but one thing the doctor had said stayed uppermost in her mind. He had delivered Vic's son. Her father? As far as she knew, her dad had been an only child. Had this man known her dad as an infant, as a little boy?

Loud words came from Vic's bedroom as the examination was concluded and the doctor opened the door. There was no mistaking which was her grandfather's voice.

"I'm not going to no hospital, so you just forget it, Hank. I'm staying right here, taking care of my campground."

"You're in no shape to take care of anything, you old goat. Use your head, what you have left of it. We ought to get an X ray of your skull. You definitely have a concussion, and you might have a fracture."

"It always did psych you out to see a little blood," Vic said, sounding stronger by the minute. "My head still works, so it ain't fractured too bad. I got to stay here and tend to things."

"I told you. You can't tend to anything until you've had time to heal. That ankle looks bad, too, swelled up like a bullfrog about to croak."

"Sprained," Vic asserted. "Nothing but a sprain. I

got a pair of crutches around here somewhere, from the time I broke my foot. Stick a piece of tape on this cut so it stops bleeding in my eye and leave me alone. The only way you're going to carry me out of here is to plant me in the ground, and I'm not ready for that yet."

Dr. Daniels gave up. "All right. Stay home, then. And stay in bed. Yell orders at someone else about what needs to be done. I guarantee you're going to have a whale of a headache for a while, and you'll be discovering bruises and aches all over your ornery hide. A man your age can't take a fall like that without taking some punishment doing it."

Steffi heard her grandfather's snapped response. "I ain't but two years older than you are, Hank Daniels."

"And I have more sense than to go climbing around on rickety ladders."

"The gutters needed cleaning out," Vic defended himself. "How'd I know that ladder was going to spill me sideways?"

"It'll teach you to wedge a ladder so it can't slide," the doctor said, with no evidence of sympathy. "I'll send you a bill."

He was out of the bedroom before Vic shouted after him. "Wasn't me that called you! I'd have come around by myself in a few minutes!"

The doctor saw Steffi standing there, listening, and grinned at her. "Don't take him too seriously, child. He's a stubborn old codger. He sounds meaner than he is. He actually has a heart like a marshmallow."

Steffi followed him out of the living quarters, incredulous. "Marshmallow? Vic? He's the meanest man I ever saw!"

Dr. Daniels paused on his way out of the building, holding the screen door ajar. "No, no, you're reading him all wrong. All that crustiness is a facade, a cover-up."

Steffi found that hard to believe. "He didn't speak to my dad for years and years. Never even sent him—or us—a postcard."

"I said he was stubborn, didn't I?" The doctor looked down into Steffi's face and his expression softened. "He thought the world of that boy. Nothing was too good for Ludwig Victor Tomaschek, you know. I was always grateful they didn't call him by that name. Skip was a good kid; I liked him, too."

"Skip?" Steffi echoed.

"That's what they called him. Skippy. Always skipping around from one place to another, never could hold still, climbing into the darndest places, hanging from the highest thing he could get hold of. Always risking his neck, though he never seemed to get more than a scrape or a bruise."

"He changed his name," Steffi said. "He had it legally changed to Larry Thomas."

The doctor's kindly face sobered. "I know. I heard he went into the movies as a stuntman. He was a good one, I'd guess. He never was afraid to try anything. I was sorry he finally had that bad accident. I read about it in the paper."

"My grandfather never even answered the letter Mom sent, telling him Dad had been hurt so bad. Nor when she sent another one saying Daddy had died."

"I expect he was so full of grief and regret he couldn't think of anything to say. He never was much of a letter writer anyway." The doctor was smiling gently.

"Grief! But he hated my dad—"

Dr. Daniels was shaking his head. "No, he didn't. Don't you ever believe that, young lady. It liked to broke Vic's heart when the boy left. He had such big hopes for him, expected him to go into a profession and make a name for himself. And when he changed his name . . . well, that was his son's final repudiation. Vic knew he'd lost him, and he sort of closed in on himself, you know. Got to be a grouchy old fellow, but his heart's in the right place."

Steffi had trouble believing that. The doctor patted her on the shoulder and started down the steps, but she followed him out to his car.

"You said you delivered his son. My dad."

"That I did. And a difficult job it was, too. He was turned the wrong way around, came out feet first, and it took a long time. Poor Margaret had one of the longest labors I ever attended, and Vic was beside himself, praying for both of them to come through it all right."

"So you knew my grandmother, too."

"Of course. Knew the whole family ever since they came to this area when I was just a brand-new physician. They married late, and having a baby at Margaret's age wasn't easy. But she came through it all right, and the baby was big and healthy. Spunky little kid, he was. Always butting heads with his daddy, once he got to be fourteen, fifteen, I guess. They'd argue, and yell at each other, and be mad for a few hours, and then they'd make up. Margaret always made them make up and apologize. At least *Skip* apologized."

"It would have meant a lot to us all," Steffi said softly as the doctor got into his wine red Porsche, "if Vic had apologized to anybody."

"I know. I know. It was always a hard thing for him to do, to speak out first and say he was wrong or he was sorry. And after Margaret died, it seemed like it was more than he could do at all. Margaret was what held Vic together, and he just couldn't do things very well without her."

Steffi rested a hand on the car door. "What did she die of, my grandmother?"

"Pneumonia. They didn't call me until it was too late. It was winter, and they were snowed in out here, and it took days for the snowplow to get around to the side roads. Vic wanted to get out his snowshoes and hike to town, but they were alone, and Margaret didn't want him to leave her by herself. She was sure she'd get better on her own. When Vic finally got desperate and came after me, we both came back in on snowshoes, but I couldn't save her. She was a lovely woman, Margaret was. I think if she'd lived, your dad and your grandpa would have gotten back together. She wouldn't have let them stay mad at each other."

Steffi felt the sting of tears. "I wish I'd known her."

"I wish so too, child. But you've still got your grandpa, and don't sell him short. He's got more heart than you think he has. You just hang in there and make him show it."

What a piece of advice, Steffi thought as the doctor's flashy little car left the campground. How on earth was she supposed to make him show anything? He scarcely communicated with her at all!

Vic didn't want any supper when she asked him, so she toasted a cheese sandwich and ate alone. She'd lost so much of her appetite that she even gave Buddy the last of the sandwich.

It was nearly dark when she cleaned up the kitchen and cautiously looked into Vic's bedroom.

He had fallen asleep, but there were lines of pain etched into his tanned face.

Steffi didn't know if she was feeling more sorry for him, or for herself. It made her sad that she'd never known her grandmother Margaret, or Vic when he was younger and happier, or even her father when they'd called him Skippy. It was hard to imagine Larry Thomas being a little boy named Skippy.

She turned away, hearing a car outside. One of the regulars coming home, or an overnighter?

She caught a glimpse of Helen disappearing out the back door and decided it must be a newcomer. Helen didn't hide from the regulars.

A wispy little man in a Forty-Niners' T-shirt came in the front door. "Evening," he said. "Can I get a campsite for the night? Saw the sign out on the main road," he added.

"Yes, we have a campsite." Steffi tried to remember what Vic would have asked. "Do you need a complete hookup? Water, electricity, and sewer?"

"All three, I guess."

The man followed her into the office.

"How many in your party?" Steffi pulled out one of the registration slips and picked up a pen.

"Eight. Me and my wife and six kids."

Steffi blinked, but wrote in the figures.

"Oh, and the dog. Does it cost extra for the dog?" the man asked.

"No. But he has to stay on a leash unless someone's right with him all the time. To clean up after him."

"The kids can walk him and do that. Oh, and they wanted me to ask: Is it too late to use the pool? They were hoping to swim yet this evening. Is it closed yet?"

"No, it's open. It hasn't been filled for very long, though, so it's not very warm."

"Oh, they won't mind that." The man signed his name to the slip Steffi pushed toward him—Bill Sadler—and wrote in his license number. Steffi took the bill he offered, punched the right figures into the cash register, then handed over his change. "I'll show you where to park," she told him.

After she'd gotten the Sadler family settled in an empty space, she came back to see Chester Taylor emerging from the office carrying a carton of cigarettes.

Through the window from the hallway she could see the counter beside the cash register. He hadn't left any money there to pay for them.

He was big and bulky and he didn't look friendly. Steffi didn't really want to speak to him, but it was clear he'd taken the cigarettes from the store.

"Did you want something?" she asked.

Chester seemed a bit disconcerted. "Uh, oh, I needed some smokes." He lifted the carton, as if she hadn't seen it already. "Nobody around, so I figured I'd pay you next time I came in."

The whole time Steffi had been here, she'd never known the Taylors to get more than one or two packs of cigarettes at a time. Had Chester just seen the opportunity to steal a whole carton?

"Just a minute," she said now. "I'll have to ask Vic how much they are by the carton. I'll be right back."

"I'm kinda in a hurry," Chester said, scowling a little.

"Well, you could just pay me the regular price it would be for individual packages," Steffi said, wondering where she got the courage to challenge him, but knowing she didn't dare let him walk out of here without paying. Vic would be furious, maybe worse than usual because his head and his ankle were hurting. "Then the next time you're in, we can refund the difference."

She walked into the office, and after a few seconds' hesitation Chester reluctantly followed her. Her mouth went dry, trying to figure out what to do if he defied her attempt to collect.

He set the carton on the counter and reached for his wallet. After inspecting its contents he made a grunting sound. "Well. Looks like I don't have quite enough to do it today."

Feeling a bit like Daniel facing the lion, Steffi reached for the carton and opened it. "So you want to buy just a couple of packs, then?"

The look he gave her shriveled her determination, but Steffi didn't say anything, and after a moment Chester slapped a bill down in front of her and picked up the two packs she'd pushed toward him.

She made change and handed it to him. "Thank you," she said.

He didn't answer, just turned and stalked out.

She hoped Vic wouldn't be laid up very long. Or that the Taylors would stay out of the store until Vic was well. She was uncomfortable around Burt, but she decided she was just plain scared of Chester.

She heard Vic's raised voice the minute she stepped into the living quarters.

"Can't anybody hear me?" Vic was bellowing.

"Yes, I'm here." Steffi went to his bedroom doorway. "I was waiting on Mr. Taylor. He was taking some cigarettes without paying for them."

"He's as bad as his kid," Vic snarled, and it was impossible to tell if his fury related to Chester or to his own pain. "You get the money?"

"Yes. I just checked in a trailer family. I put them in space twelve. Eight of them, with a dog."

Vic thrashed around on the bed, punching his pillow. "Didn't Doc leave me something for this headache?"

"No. He said you'd have a headache, but it would be better if you didn't have any pain medication tonight."

Vic punched the pillow again. "Doggone quack. Should have got somebody else."

"Dr. Daniels was the closest one. We thought we should get someone as fast as possible." Steffi stared at him, trying to reconcile this disagreeable old man with the father who had given her own dad everything he wanted when Larry was a little boy called Skippy.

Vic slumped back. "Did they pay cash?"

"Yes."

He groaned. Was he hurting, or only frustrated that he couldn't manage things himself? "Don't you try to pump any propane. It's nothing to fool with."

"I won't," Steffi assured him.

"If their dog makes a mess, they're responsible for cleaning it up."

"I told them," Steffi said.

"By tomorrow that Vail fellow's time will be up unless he pays again."

"All right."

Vic glared at her as if she were the cause of his dis-
comfort. Then, abruptly, he closed his eyes, shutting
her out.

Steffi waited another few minutes, but he seemed to
have fallen asleep.

She wondered what it would have been like if
Margaret had still been there. Margaret, she was sure,
would have welcomed her. Hugged her, and baked her
chocolate-chip cookies.

She turned out the light in the office, leaving one on
by the night registration window for latecomers, just in
case her newly painted sign drew in anyone else. She
supposed she ought to go out and put the plastic tarp
back over the pool, but the Sadler kids were still whoop-
ing and hollering and having a good time, and she hated
to cut them off. Their mother, a woman twice the size of
her husband, had promised to stay with them as long as
they were in the pool.

Steffi felt very tired. She decided to go to bed.
Heaven only knew what she'd be called upon to do the
next day if Vic still had to stay in bed.

She was glad when Buddy padded after her and
hoisted his big black body up beside her in the bed. She
spoke softly to him in the dark.

"I'm spoiling you. I'll bet Vic won't let you sleep with
him after I'm gone."

The thought made her giggle softly, and she hugged
the dog against her as she drifted off to sleep.

10

Though Casey reported that the pool had warmed up enough to be quite comfortable, Steffi didn't have time to try it out.

Vic had managed to get to the bathroom, but the effort had left him limp as Buddy's tail after he'd been scolded. The old man collapsed once more onto his bed, where his ankle ached and his head hurt and he felt generally terrible.

Not that he told this to Steffi. She could tell by looking at him.

Elwood and Oliver stopped in to see him. Helen brought a tuna casserole. Mrs. Montoni delivered a chocolate cream pie. Mrs. Johnson presented them with a loaf of fresh bread.

The food was a good idea, because Steffi didn't have time to fix much of anything. She'd had no idea there was so much to do, running a campground.

There were suppliers to deal with. The bakery man, the dairy truck, the local farmer who kept them stocked with eggs. The man who refilled the propane tank came and had to have a receipt signed for the delivery.

Floors had to be swept in the office, the hallway, the laundry room, and the porch. Vic asked if she'd gotten the fingerprints off the frozen food display case, so Steffi got the glass cleaner and did that. Then she noticed that the front window of the office looked pretty dingy, so she cleaned that, also. There were outgoing letters to be carried all the way out to the mailbox. The rest rooms and showers for the use of the campers had to be cleaned.

By the time she'd finished those, Steffi was hot and tired. Mom hadn't told her she'd wind up scrubbing toilets and showers for a summer vacation.

Of course this wasn't supposed to be a vacation. She'd been sent to her grandfather because Mom couldn't take a child along on location.

She was heading for the shed, carrying her brushes and buckets, when Casey called out to her.

"Hey, Steffi, want to go swimming?"

She waited for him to catch up to her. "I don't know if I dare. Vic's been alone for quite a while now. I'll have to check on him first."

"Okay. I'll come along." He lowered his voice. "I just saw something kind of interesting."

"Oh, what?"

"Mr. Vail was sitting in front of his rig, reading,

when Chester Taylor got in his pickup and drove out. Vail got up, very casually, you know, and wandered back toward the lake. Only he didn't go to his boat. He looked around—I was watching from inside our trailer, where he couldn't see me—and he started poking around Taylor's trailer."

Steffi stopped walking. "What do you mean? How poking around?"

"Just looking, at first. Peeked in a window. Lifted the cover off the junk Chester's got stacked behind the trailer. And then he looked around again, making sure nobody was watching, and he went inside. The really interesting part is—" Casey paused for dramatic effect. "He picked the lock to do it."

Steffi's jaw dropped. "He broke in?"

"He broke in. He was in there quite a while—ten, fifteen minutes, anyway. I wanted to sneak back and look in, but I was afraid I'd get caught. I don't have any doubts about what he was doing, though."

"What?" Steffi demanded, bewildered.

"Searching the place. It's such a little place, he must have turned everything inside-out. He wasn't carrying anything when he came out, and he walked straight back to his own rig."

"Searching for what? Why would he think Chester Taylor would have something worth stealing? He's got an old trailer, an old pickup, and there isn't room to hide much of anything."

"I don't know, but it makes me wonder if Helen's right. If he's a detective."

"Shouldn't he have a search warrant, if he's a detective?" Steffi wondered.

"Sure, legally. But don't you watch crime shows? Private detectives and even cops are always snooping without search warrants. You have to have probable cause to get a judge to sign one in the first place." Casey looked around at the sound of a motor, in time to see Kurt Vail driving out. The man waved and halted beside them.

"I'm going into town. Need anything?"

"No, thanks," they both said in unison.

"Okay. See you later," Vail said, and drove away.

When Steffi looked back at Casey, he had an odd expression on his face. "What?" she demanded.

"I was just thinking. Chester's only been gone half an hour, so he's not likely to be back for a while. Burt is working. And Mr. Vail didn't relock the trailer when he came out. Nobody's moving around this time of day— they're watching soap operas, or reading, or taking naps. I'll bet nobody'd notice if I went over and looked around myself."

"That would be illegal, too, wouldn't it?" Guessing that he might be about to ask her to join him, Steffi said quickly, "I'd better check on Vic."

"I think Helen's right, he's a detective," Casey went on. "He's not really acting like a tourist on vacation. Oh, he's been fishing a few times, but he's not working at it nearly as hard as he is at snooping and asking questions."

"You could get in real trouble if you went into Taylor's trailer. Maybe Vail is just a thief. Why would a detective be interested in someone who doesn't have any more than they do?"

She remembered, though, how the Chapmans and

the Taylors, as well as Helen, had reacted to Kurt Vail. "What would a genuine detective be doing in this little old campground?"

"Who knows? Helen's nervous about strangers, but most of the time she doesn't seem crazy. Just because she's old doesn't rule out that there might be something she doesn't want known about herself."

"Like where she came from, and what her real name is, and the name of her dog," Steffi confirmed. "But what would he be investigating? He didn't come here looking for an old lady and an ugly dog." And what did the Taylors and the Chapmans have to fear from an investigator?

"Who knows? Dad thinks there's something fishy about Chester Taylor. He's up to something. Maybe all that talk about his bad back isn't true. He's drawing disability for that, you know. If a private investigator caught him hauling a boat out of the water, for instance, they might cut off those payments. Dad saw him a few days ago, lifting the battery out of his truck and putting a new one in. He didn't act like someone with a bad back."

Steffi told him about Chester trying to walk away with a whole carton of cigarettes. "I wouldn't put it past him to cheat anybody on anything." Her steps slowed as she reached the front porch. "I better check on Vic. You aren't really going to break into Taylor's trailer, are you?"

"I wouldn't have to break in. It's unlocked. All I know is I don't like him. I don't care much for Burt, either, but I hate the way his dad yells at him and knocks him around."

And what are you afraid of, from a detective? Steffi wanted to ask, but didn't quite dare. "If Mr. Vail *is* a detective, he's probably carrying ID that would prove it, wouldn't you think?"

Casey nodded. "We'll have to think of a way to get a look at his ID," he said. "Maybe we could get him to go swimming, and check it out when he leaves his wallet in his pants' pocket."

"Lots of luck," Steffi said. "His rig is right in plain sight of the pool, and the door's on this side."

There was a muffled bellow from inside the building, and Steffi jumped. "I better go," she said, and ran inside.

Vic had gotten out of bed, tried to use the crutches, and fallen on them, landing in a tangle in the bathroom doorway.

He glared at her. "You'd think a person could get a drink without killing himself, but no, nobody cares if they don't hear me," he said.

It was unfair, since she'd been outside doing *his* usual chores up to the last five minutes. But Steffi reminded herself that he was hurting and frustrated, and that was why he was even more unreasonable than usual. Even Daddy had been cross when he was laid up with a broken leg so he couldn't work.

"Let me help you up," she offered, but he waved her away.

"Pull that chair over here. I can hoist myself on that," he snapped, and Steffi obeyed.

"I'll get you some water and put it on the table by the bed, so you won't have to get up next time," she offered as he stumped back to his own room.

She put ice in a tall glass, wishing she had one that

was insulated so it would stay cold longer, and brought it to him. It was then that she saw the photograph on the nightstand, turned so that he could see it from the bed.

The face was smiling, young, and reminded her of her father.

Steffi studied it, not thinking that perhaps her grandfather would object to her interest in his private possessions. "That's my grandmother, isn't it? Margaret. She looks like a very nice person."

"She's dead," Vic said, thumping his pillow. "Everybody I cared about is dead."

"For me, too," Steffi said softly, still looking at her grandmother's portrait. "I wish I had known her. Daddy's gone, and I don't have any other family, except Mom."

And you, she thought, but she couldn't say it. It was obvious he didn't consider her part of his family, which wasn't surprising after he'd disowned her father years earlier.

"Are you hungry yet?" she asked, though it was still too early for supper.

"No," Vic said shortly.

Clearly he wanted her to leave him alone, yet Steffi hesitated. "Do you want me to bring the TV in here, so you can watch it?"

"Wouldn't work," Vic said, not looking at her. "It has to be hooked to the antenna, or it wouldn't get anything."

"Maybe Mr. Chapman could put a longer lead-in wire on it," Steffi said, and then turned away before he could add a negative comment to that, too.

That afternoon and evening, four new rigs came in.

They all had kids who wanted to swim. They'd seen the new sign and decided to stop even though the Hidden Valley RV Park wasn't listed in the campground guide. The parents all bought bread and milk and eggs and ice-cream bars, keeping Steffi busy in the office/store. Two of the mothers wanted change for the laundry equipment, and there was a disagreement between them as to whether the first person there got to use the washer until she had done three loads, or if the other lady was entitled to get a turn in between.

Steffi wasn't sure what Vic would have said, and she wasn't inclined to go and ask him, so she settled it the best she could on her own. "It's always been first come, first served, as far as I know. Until the first person is finished."

"But it says the laundry is only open until nine," the second woman argued. "By the time she's done, it'll close before I get mine done."

"I'll leave it unlocked until you finish," Steffi said. Though it was not what the woman wanted, she ungraciously accepted that and stomped out, grumbling. Steffi wondered if Vic had gotten around to ordering the part the second washing machine needed. Of course he wasn't in any shape to install it, even if it came, she reflected, returning to the office where one of the fathers wanted change for the phone.

The lady from the green camper was waiting for her attention. "This milk you sold me is sour," she announced.

Steffi sniffed at the carton. "Yes, it is. Help yourself to another one," she said, hoping that was the correct response.

No sooner had that customer left when three children, in dripping swimsuits, entered. One of them was hopping on one foot and dripping blood from the other one.

"Jody stepped on a piece of glass," the older boy said. "She needs a bandage on it."

Inspection revealed a cut too large for a Band-Aid. Steffi opened a box of gauze from the grocery shelves, sprayed the area with antiseptic (also from the sale shelves), and taped the whole thing over. "You'll have to stay out of the pool for now," she said to the little girl. "Where did you step on the glass?"

"Billy Ray broke a pop bottle on the cement," Jody said.

"You aren't supposed to have food or drink, especially not in glass containers, in the pool area. Didn't you read the sign? I'd better get a broom and make sure it's all cleaned up."

As she was on her way out—having taken time to lock the office behind her—she met Helen, carrying a covered dish while protecting her hands with pot holders. The drifting steamy aroma reminded Steffi that she was hungry, and it was well past suppertime. Vic! She'd gotten so busy she'd forgotten him!

"I could see you didn't have time to cook," Helen said, "with all the new customers. They aren't likely to be detectives, do you think, with all those children? I'll dish some of this up for Vic, shall I?"

"Yes, please. And thank you, Helen." Steffi gave her a tired but grateful smile.

The glass was swept up, the boys still in the pool were admonished that there was a rule against running on the wet cement, and Steffi returned to the office. Burt Taylor was leaning against the door.

"You didn't have to lock it," he told her. "I would have got what I wanted and left the money on the counter."

"Sorry. Vic wants me to lock it unless I'm in there. What was it you needed?"

"Cigarettes. Two packs," Burt said, following her inside.

"Sorry. It's illegal to sell tobacco to anyone who's underage."

The smile slid off Burt's face. "They're for my dad."

Right after his father had just bought two packs? A tremor went through her, but Steffi held her ground. "It's against the law. He'll have to buy them himself."

"So he'll be mad at me for not getting them." Burt sounded as ugly as he looked.

"I don't make the laws," Steffi reminded him. She wasn't sure if Vic would have given them to him or not, but she was sure about kids not being allowed to buy cigarettes.

Burt spun on his heel and left, fuming. He almost knocked Casey over as they met in the doorway, without apology.

"Excuse me, too," Casey muttered. "Hey, Steffi, the light is burned out in the men's room. If you'll get me a bulb, I'll replace it."

That, too, was chosen from the stock on the shelves, and she asked Casey about more lead-in wire for the TV.

"I think Dad may have some left from ours," Casey said.

She hesitated, then asked, "Did you do it?"

He didn't pretend not to know what she was talking about.

"It's hard to tell if the place was searched or not, just by looking in the door. Chester and Burt aren't exactly housekeepers. There are dirty dishes, dirty clothes on the floors and the furniture. I didn't see anything suspicious, though."

Well, at least he hadn't been caught in the act. She was relieved about that.

By the time Steffi finally was able to turn out the lights in the office and lock up for the night, she had not eaten and she was ready for bed. Buddy's mournful gaze suggested he had not been fed, either.

The remains of the casserole—chicken and dumplings—had been left in the top of a double boiler on a burner turned low. Steffi ate it directly from the pan, then gave what little remained to the dog, along with a cupful of his kibble.

"I don't know if Helen is batty or not," she told Buddy quietly, "but she's a nice lady and a good cook."

Buddy wagged agreement.

When she peeked in on Vic, he had fallen asleep. His reading glasses were still in one hand, and after a moment's hesitation Steffi carefully removed them without waking him and placed them beside his empty water glass. Only then did she notice what he'd been reading.

A Bible.

It made her feel strange to think of Vic reading a Bible. True, he always said grace before meals, but somehow it was hard to think of him as a religious man. He was so curt, so short-tempered, so unforgiving.

The leather-bound book had slid down beside him. She picked it up, then on impulse carried it out to the kitchen instead of placing it on the nightstand. After she'd refilled the glass with ice water, in case he woke up thirsty in the night, Steffi sat at the table and looked at the Bible.

In faded gold letters was a name: *Margaret Tomaschek*. It had belonged to her grandmother.

Steffi cast a glance toward Vic's bedroom, but he was fast asleep. She opened the cover and began to look through it.

Inside, there was an inscription: *To my dearest Maggie, from your loving Victor.*

Maggie. He had called his wife Maggie. His *dearest* Maggie. Inside of Steffi, something shifted, changing her perception of Vic ever so slightly.

11

Your loving Victor. Steffi read it again in a whisper. What had he been like in the days when he had written that? When he and his Maggie were young. How would it have changed her own life if they'd been around as grandparents when she was a little girl? Would Vic have liked her if he hadn't been so angry with her father?

Steffi turned the pages, so well-worn the gilt was almost gone from their edges. Her grandmother had read this book often.

Some passages were highlighted as she leafed through the pages. And about two-thirds of the way through them, she came upon a treasure.

Steffi found an entire family that she had never heard about.

Mom had talked a little about *her* family. Her father, a machinist, had died before Steffi was born. Her mother was a dim memory, an old lady who smelled of peppermints and fresh-baked bread. There had been a brother, Ned, who was lost in a boating accident on the Russian River when he was a boy. There had been various aunts and uncles, none of whom Steffi remembered meeting.

She knew her father and *his* father had quarreled many years ago, that they had been estranged for more years than Steffi had been alive. Once in a while, very rarely, Larry Thomas—or Ludwig Tomaschek, as he had been—had mentioned his mother, though Steffi had never known her name was Margaret. And now here was Margaret's family, listed in the form of a family tree.

Steffi's grandmother had had four brothers and a sister. Their names, and those of Margaret's parents, were written out, along with the names of the people her siblings had married, and the names of their children and their children's children.

Some of those children's children's birthdates were only a few years before Steffi's own. If Margaret had lived a little longer, might there have been even more children's births listed, ones her own age or younger?

Cousins, or second cousins, Steffi thought. Where were they now? Some of them were so close to her own age!

Would Vic tell her where they were? Would she dare to ask him?

She lingered over the page where her grandparents' marriage had been recorded. June 2, in Traverse City, Michigan. It gave a birthdate and birthplace for each of them.

These relatives began to come alive in Steffi's mind. How strange, that she had all these relatives, and she'd never known about them!

Did they know about her?

Would they want to know her?

How could she find them, if Vic hadn't kept in touch with them, either? Or if he refused to tell her?

The light over the kitchen table was not a good one, and her eyes were beginning to ache, trying to read the somewhat faded ink on the family tree. But she wanted to see it all before she gave the Bible back to her grandfather.

And here was the page for her father's family.

Born to Victor and Margaret Tomaschek: Ludwig Victor Tomaschek. January 17, 1960, in Moon Bay, Michigan.

There was no hospital in the little town. Had Dad been born here at home, then? And in the middle of the winter, had there been a snowstorm, like the one when Margaret had died of pneumonia? Had Vic been able to get a doctor to come that time?

Oh, of course he had. Dr. Daniels had said he'd delivered Skippy.

Steffi's gaze moved on down the page, to the branch of the family tree beneath her father's name.

There was no name filled in where her mother's should have been, as Ludwig's wife. But below that, written in pencil so faintly that she could hardly read it, Steffi saw the word *daughter*.

Who had written it in? Margaret? Had Margaret known she had a granddaughter? But it hadn't been entered in ink, and she wasn't sure the handwriting was the same.

There was no date written in for Margaret's death. There had been only Vic to write it, and perhaps he was unable to put that loss into writing in the family records. So Steffi wasn't sure if her grandmother had died before or after she herself had been born. Mom hadn't met her, only Vic after Margaret was gone.

She hoped Margaret had known about her.

In the adjoining bedroom, Vic made a sound. Of distress, or pain, maybe.

Steffi started to close the book, feeling a moment of panic at the possibility that he might catch her reading through what he might think of as none of her business. But there was no further sound from the bedroom, and she got up quickly and brought a pad and pencil back to the table. Before she returned the Bible she wanted to copy down the names of those relatives who were probably still alive, in case she never got another chance.

Somehow, with Vic's cooperation or without it, she would find them if she could.

Then she carried the Bible back to its place on the nightstand, walking very carefully so that she wouldn't wake Vic.

The list she kept, hiding it in her dresser drawer under her T-shirts.

When she went to bed, she thought about those young cousins, remembered some of their names— David, Kathie, Chris, Larrilyn, Nicole, Samantha, Saul, Matthew, and Sarah—there were others, but she couldn't remember them. She tried to make faces come to match the names, but of course she had no idea what any of them looked like. But I will, Steffi thought excitedly. Maybe they'll be pleased to have another cousin.

Her dreams were pleasant, about having a big family reunion and all the relatives kissing her in greeting.

It wasn't even disappointing when she woke to find that it was Buddy licking her cheek, not kisses from cousins. Steffi smiled and put an arm around the big dog's neck before she dozed off again.

The following days took on a pattern. Up early, in the store to sell supplies to campers who were leaving. Sweeping hall and porch and laundry room. Fixing meals.

If he had any appreciation, Vic didn't show it. He grunted over most of her offerings, yet he always ate everything she took him. Steffi decided she didn't have time to worry about it.

Bo Chapman came over and rigged up a new lead-in wire for the TV so it could be moved into Vic's bedroom. Oliver brought a book he thought Vic might enjoy. Elwood brought an exquisite little model of a sailing ship to put on Vic's windowsill. The ladies continued to arrive daily with gifts of food, and the Montoni children came with a cheese glass filled with tiny wildflowers.

Steffi didn't hear Vic thanking anyone, so she did it. It certainly made her job easier, not to have to worry about food.

The part came for the washing machine. Casey brought the mail up, and plunked it down on the counter.

"I wish we knew how to fix it," Steffi said. "People could really use another washer. The Pellinis have decided to stay on through the weekend, and their kids are changing clothes every time they swim. She asked if we couldn't get the other machine operating."

Casey had opened the package and was reading the instructions that came with it. "Maybe we could figure it out," he mused.

"And screw it up and have Vic hanging us up by our thumbs as soon as he can get out of bed?" Steffi asked, alarmed.

"Hmm. How about if I take this over to Elwood and ask if he might be able to put it in? He's pretty good mechanically."

Steffi had sorted out the letters and found one from her mother. "Sure, ask him," she said, ripping open the envelope.

It was a good letter. It said Audri missed her, and that she was so busy being both an assistant to the director and playing the second lead that she hardly had time to breathe. *But I love it,* her mother wrote. *I never dreamed anything else could be as satisfying as acting.*

Well, maybe that was a step forward, Steffi thought. If Audri decided she liked doing a regular job with a regular salary, that would be helpful. Except, of course, that she'd have to be on location with the director, wherever he went, which probably would mean Steffi would still be left behind.

We're going to be near Albuquerque for a few days, the end of next week, her mother had written. *How about writing to me there, care of General Delivery? Is there a phone number where I could call you—does the old goat have a phone? The operator couldn't give me a listing for him, but how do you run a campground or take reservations without a phone?*

He put in a pay phone, Steffi could have told her. And Vic didn't worry about reservations since most of his customers lived right there already. She'd answer the letter tonight, to make sure it got there before her mother left Albuquerque, and put in the number of the pay phone.

Casey and Elwood returned before noon to announce that the washing machine was now fixed. Mrs. Pellini showed up half an hour later asking for quarters to run three loads of clothes, and to wish audibly that they had a second dryer, as well.

"The one we have is big enough to handle several loads at once," Steffi pointed out.

"But somebody else is using it now," Mrs. Pellini said. "I can't mix our clothes with theirs."

"It should be finishing up by the time yours are washed," Steffi said.

She wondered if Vic went through this kind of thing every day, saying the same things over and over to different people.

In the middle of the afternoon, while she was checking over the bread order so she could sign for it, and wishing she could join that shrieking mob of kids in the pool, Steffi looked up to see Casey approaching with a look of excitement.

"What's up?" she demanded as soon as the bread man had gone.

Casey smacked a flat leather folder onto the counter. "Look what I found. Right on the edge of the driveway, over by Mr. Vail's camper."

She didn't understand until Casey flipped open the case.

"FBI! He *is* a cop! What on earth is he doing here?"

"Who, that Vail guy?"

They hadn't heard Herbert Johnson come in, but without an invitation he stepped up beside Casey and turned the leather case so he could read it more easily. "Not after any of us, I shouldn't think. FBI doesn't go after small fry. Chances are he's just on vacation. Even FBI agents must take some time off."

"So he's been nosy just because it's a habit?" Casey asked, frowning a little.

"If he's a federal agent," Steffi contributed slowly, "I'd expect him to be more subtle, not make everyone suspect he's the law. Everybody in camp has suspected him."

Mr. Johnson laughed. "Lots of guilty consciences, eh? Well, mine's clean. Worst trouble I ever had with the law was a speeding ticket, and I paid that a long time ago. Steffi, my wife wants to know if you've got any strawberry Jell-O."

"It's right here," Casey offered, and got it off the shelf behind him.

They waited until the man had paid for it and left before they returned their attention to the ID folder and badge. "Federal Bureau of Investigation," Steffi read aloud. "Mr. Johnson's right, don't you think? If he were here on business, it would have to be something pretty serious?"

"We'll have to give it back," Casey said, nodding, "but I wanted you to see it first."

Steffi was thoughtful. "Isn't it kind of strange that he'd drop it where you'd find it? Or somebody would. Right on the edge of the road?"

Casey considered. "Careless, for a cop, right? Maybe—maybe he wanted us to find it. Maybe he *wanted* us to know he's with the FBI."

"Then why wouldn't he mention it, right out?" Steffi wondered.

They couldn't figure it out. When Casey returned the official folder, Mr. Vail thanked him but made no explanation.

The word got around. One by one, people drifted through the office or the store or by the pool where Steffi was watching the swimmers, not daring to join them in case new campers showed up.

"I knew it!" Helen said. "I said he was a detective, remember?"

Oliver and Elwood, picking up their papers, joked about it. "I knew they'd catch up with us sooner or later, Ollie," Elwood said. "All this high living we've been doing, they were bound to notice it in Washington."

"Next thing you know, they'll be getting a court order to open our safety-deposit boxes," Oliver cackled.

Even Mrs. Evans, to whom Steffi delivered a quart of milk as Vic usually did once a week, had already heard the news. "Isn't that exciting? I don't think I ever met an FBI man before."

When Bo Chapman came home from work, stopping to deliver the fresh produce Steffi had requested, Casey told him the minute he got out of his pickup.

Bo stood still for a moment, then said, "Nothing to do with us, son. You didn't have strawberries on your list, Steffi, but these just came in and I thought you might like some."

"Great," Steffi said, thanking him. And then, when Bo had gone, she looked Casey in the eye.

"Do we know each other well enough for me to ask?" she wanted to know.

"Ask what?" Casey sounded innocent.

"You were afraid it was something to do with you when Helen first guessed he was a detective. It made you and your dad both nervous. And Helen, and the Taylors, too. Do I get to know what's going on? This campground can't be full of people who are hiding from the police."

For a moment she didn't think he was going to answer. Then his shoulders slumped, almost in relief. "I guess we can trust you to know. If it was a private detective—"

She remembered the joking remark he'd once made about having robbed a bank in Detroit. It *had* been a joke, hadn't it?

Casey drew in a deep breath. "You asked if I finished out the school year here. I couldn't. We couldn't risk getting any of my records from home for the local school. We don't want anyone from there to know where we are. We don't know yet what we're going to do when school starts in September."

Steffi felt tense and apprehensive. "Why?"

"Because, technically, when my folks got divorced, Mom got custody of me. I tried living with her for a while, but I couldn't stand it, Steffi. I don't like the kind of people she runs around with. The kind of men who kept coming to the house. The way she . . . drinks. So I told my dad, and he tried again to get custody of me. When Mom's lawyer managed to keep that from happening . . . well, one night my mom and I had a big fight, and I ran away to Dad's and told him I couldn't stand it any longer . . . so we packed up the next day and left town. Dad quit his job, and we took off. I guess we've been running ever since."

Steffi was stunned. "What a terrible way to live! Do you really think there's a chance Mr. Vail is a detective looking for you?"

"No. Not anymore. We know now he's FBI, and they only deal with federal crimes. Felonies. He couldn't have been hired by my mom to track us down. She did hire a guy once, and we had to pack up and move then. Dad's had to take different kinds of jobs from what he used to do, and he earns less money. It bothers him to do something that's against a court order. But he says it's worth it to protect me. I want to stay with him. I'm old enough so that lots of judges would let me decide for myself, but not the one who has jurisdiction back home. He's due to retire soon, a friend of Dad's wrote to tell us that. So maybe when someone new is elected this fall, I can go back to court and fight for the right to stay with my dad."

Steffi swallowed. "I hope you can. So you can go back to school, and your father can work at a better job."

"Yeah." Casey suddenly grinned. "Maybe I can just stay home and study on my own. Dad's a pretty good teacher."

She wasn't the only one with problems, Steffi reflected as Casey left. She didn't know if she'd want to trade with Casey, to worry about private detectives and an unreasonable judge and a parent she didn't want to live with.

She began to run water into the sink to wash the

asparagus Bo had just brought, and unwrapped the pork chops for supper. Dad would be proud of her, the way she'd taken over cooking and was getting Vic to eat things he'd never eaten before. Even if her grandfather had never yet said a nice thing about her cooking, he sometimes ate seconds, which seemed a good sign.

While the potatoes were baking along with the chops, Steffi went back to the laundry to fold the load of clothes she'd left in the dryer. She tried not to leave anything in a machine for very long because so many people needed to use the equipment.

Helen was there, with Barkley, putting a load in the washer that had just been fixed. Technically, dogs weren't supposed to be in the laundry room, but Steffi couldn't see that the ugly little mutt was hurting anything. Besides, Buddy went everywhere he wanted to go, and Vic didn't mind him in the store or the house except when the dog smelled of rotten fish.

Helen turned to greet her with a smile, poking at her bird's nest hair, which was wilder looking than ever. Some days she remembered to comb it, but not today.

"How's Vic doing? I made a lemon pie. Would you each like a slice of it?"

"That would be great," Steffi said. "I think he's sore, and his head aches, but he's no worse, anyway."

She had just put all the clothes into the basket when Helen's dog barked sharply behind her.

Steffi turned as Helen said, "Shush, Barkley, other people can use this. . . ."

Her voice trailed off when Kurt Vail loomed up in the doorway.

"Mrs. Risku," he began, "I just went in your trailer—"

He didn't get to finish. The old lady stared at him, her mouth opening and closing soundlessly. And then she fainted dead away, sinking to the floor before Steffi could try to catch her.

12

Kurt Vail was beside her in an instant. "Mrs. Risku! Are you all right?"

Already Helen was opening her eyes, though they were unfocused. She moaned.

"What happened? Do you have a bad heart?"

"I think you scared her," Steffi said, kneeling beside the old lady and reaching for her hand. "Helen, can you hear me?"

Barkley leaped into his mistress's face, licking at her cheek, and began to bark again, until finally Helen stirred and pushed him away, trying to sit up. Mr. Vail helped her and stayed kneeling with a supporting arm around her.

"What did I do? Why should I have scared her? I only

wanted to tell her I smelled something burning and went into her trailer to turn the fire off under the potatoes she was frying. They're pretty well scorched. I don't think she can eat them."

Helen moaned again, and tears slid down her wrinkled, papery cheeks.

"She's afraid of you because you're a detective," Steffi blurted, hoping no serious damage had been done.

His eyebrows went up. "I'm a federal agent. I don't go around terrorizing old ladies."

Steffi's own mind was beginning to function again. "I think she was afraid because you heard her call Barkley by name."

Mr. Vail withdrew his supporting arm; Helen didn't seem to need it anymore. "What's that got to do with anything?"

Steffi waited for Helen to explain, but the old lady simply sat there, wiping her eyes and trying to hold her dog at bay. Barkley wasn't used to seeing her on the floor, and was eager to comfort her with his rough pink tongue.

"She didn't want anyone to know Barkley's name," Steffi said finally. "She said if you knew, you'd recognize her even if she's using a different name from her real one."

Maybe it was time it was all out in the open. If there was something for Helen to be frightened of, perhaps the truth would clarify the problem and something could be done to reassure her. And Mr. Vail had already heard Barkley's name spoken, so that wasn't a secret any longer.

Mr. Vail mentally digested this confusing information.

"Is Barkley's name supposed to mean something to me? Or *her* name, even?"

"I didn't think it was illegal," Helen murmured. "I didn't change my name to try to cheat anyone. Just to keep Eunice from finding me."

Mr. Vail, still crouched on the floor, looked to Steffi, his eyebrows going up again. "Who's Eunice?"

"She's her daughter. I don't think she likes her daughter."

"It would be just like her to send a detective after me," Helen asserted, pulling herself together. "I kept waiting and waiting for you to arrest me. . . ."

"Whoa!" Mr. Vail drew back. "I'm not here to arrest you, Mrs. Risku. I'm not a policeman or even a private detective, I'm a federal agent, and I only followed you over here to tell you I had to go in your trailer and turn off your stove because you were burning up your potatoes. I didn't want them to set the whole place on fire."

Helen's expression changed. "My supper! I left the burner on under my supper?"

"It doesn't matter," Steffi said quickly. "We'll share ours with you." It wouldn't hurt Vic to eat only one chop instead of the two she'd planned. And the potatoes were big ones; Steffi would split one with her.

"Eunice said I was always forgetting to turn off a burner or the water or leaving the refrigerator door ajar. It's not so, I hardly ever do those things. I don't need to be in a rest home."

"Of course you don't," Steffi reassured her.

Helen seemed to become aware that she was sprawled on the floor, and she pulled her skirt down over her knees and attempted to get to her feet.

"They don't let you keep pets in the nursing home," she said. "And I won't leave Barkley. We've been companions for such a long time, years and years, and I like him a lot more than I like Eunice or that sour man she's married to. I knew she'd try to find me and put me in a rest home. . . ."

"But she didn't," Steffi told her. "Mr. Vail didn't come looking for you. Nobody's going to put you in a rest home, or take Barkley away from you." She hoped she was speaking the truth.

Kurt Vail got to his feet and lifted Helen as if she weighed no more than Barkley. He eased her into the only chair. "Rest a minute," he suggested, "until you feel stronger. I have to go, but I assure you, Mrs. Risku, you're in no danger from me. Even if I knew your daughter, I wouldn't tell her where you are."

Helen looked up into his face in dawning hope. "You wouldn't?"

"I wouldn't. She doesn't sound very nice."

"She isn't," Helen said flatly. "Not since she grew up. She used to be a nice little girl, but that was such a long time ago."

"I've got to run," Mr. Vail said, more to Steffi than to the old lady. "Can you see to her?"

"Sure," Steffi agreed. So that's what it had been about, the hiding and changing her name, and being afraid of strangers who might be detectives.

Helen wasn't so batty after all. Who would want to be put in a rest home without her beloved dog?

Steffi decided she didn't like Eunice, either.

After a few minutes, Helen felt well enough to go home, Barkley frisking at her side. Steffi promised to bring her a plate of supper as soon as it was cooked, and as she carried her laundry basket back to Vic's quarters she paused to look out through the front screened door.

Kurt Vail was sitting in his lawn chair beside his camper. He wasn't even reading, he was just sitting there. So why the big hurry to get out of the laundry room?

Scowling, feeling as if having one thing explained only made other things more baffling, Steffi watched as several vehicles drove in. People coming home from work. The Parkers, Mr. Montoni.

"Can't anybody hear me?"

The bellow, muffled though it was by several walls, sent Steffi hurrying toward Vic's bedroom.

"Yes, I'm here. I was bringing the laundry. Did you need something?" She always felt out of breath and tense when her grandfather shouted for her. He still had never called her by name, though. Somehow it was more intimidating to have him yell without using her name.

"I smell meat burning. Aren't you paying attention to what you're cooking?"

His disagreeable tone made her want to just leave him there, alone, but she kept her own voice civil. She hoped he didn't notice that she sounded shaky.

"No, it isn't burning. It has about ten more minutes to cook. I have to take some of it over to Helen, too, but I'll dish yours up first."

He glared at her. "Why do you have to take some to Helen?"

"She forgot she was frying potatoes and they

scorched. I told her we'd share. She made a lemon pie and offered to give us each a piece of it."

Vic grunted. "You're sure it's all right? It smells like it's burning."

"Maybe some fat dripped on the bottom of the pan," Steffi said, and left before she could make a comment on how unpleasant he was.

She could have said something to her father. When he got grouchy, she or her mother would call him "sour-puss," or "crabby," and make him laugh.

Nothing seemed to make Vic laugh, or even smile. How different things would be between them if Vic weren't so determined to reject her! For a moment she admitted how important it would be to her if Vic wanted her to be part of his family. But clearly he didn't want any such thing.

She brought Vic a tray, watched him inspect the butter melting on the baked potato, poke the asparagus with a cautious fork, and then bow his head for grace.

What did God think of Vic? Was it enough to say grace and occasionally read the Bible, while he was still hateful in so many other ways?

There was no way of knowing. She covered a plate to carry to Helen and walked past Kurt Vail. He smiled at her, and she said "Hi," and delivered the hot plate at the next trailer. Buddy galloped out of the woods wagging his tail at the aroma from the plate.

"This isn't for you, Buddy. Get down," Steffi told him. Barkley leaped excitedly around her feet when Helen opened the door.

"Smells delicious, dear. Oh, look, Barkley, there's a bone! You can have a bone, if you'll just be patient!"

When would Vic throw *her* a bone? A smile, a thank

you, speaking her name? Anything to show he knew she was there.

Steffi left Helen and Barkley to enjoy their supper and stepped out into the cooling evening with Buddy trotting beside her. Up at the pool there were children's voices, and from across the road at the Montonis the aroma of barbecuing hamburgers wafted toward Steffi.

She heard feet beside her and looked around to see Burt Taylor. He was in his dirty coveralls, and there was black grease under his fingernails.

"Is it true?" he demanded of her without so much as a greeting. "Is that Vail guy an FBI agent?"

He spoke in a low tone. Kurt Vail probably couldn't hear him from where he remained sitting beside his rig twenty yards away.

"Yes. Casey found his ID."

"You see it?" Burt asked.

"Yes."

"Funny he'd drop something like that," Burt observed.

"I guess federal agents are human, the same as anyone else," Steffi suggested.

Or he wanted it to be known that he was an agent. She didn't say that to Burt, though. Helen and the Chapmans weren't the only ones who had reacted to the idea that Vail might be a detective.

"He ever say what he was doing here, in this crummy RV park?"

To her own surprise, Steffi bridled. "It's not so crummy. It's a decent place for people who can't afford anything fancier. Vic does the best he can with it. No doubt Mr. Vail needs a vacation, same as anyone else."

"Huh," Burt said, and turned around and headed back to his own trailer.

So he'd come over just to verify that Vail was an officer of the law? Hmm. Steffi attempted to digest that. Had Burt been up to something illegal? But a federal agent didn't deal with penny-ante stuff, did he?

Vic had nearly finished his supper when she got back, so Steffi dished up her own food and ate at the kitchen table. Buddy lay beside her, waiting for his own share, ignoring the dog food in his dish. Three times she got up to check in new customers, so her meal was cold by the time she got to finish it. She was almost too tired to care.

As she took the last bite, Vic rapped loudly on the floor beside his bed with one of the crutches, causing Buddy to prick up his ears.

Vic knew she was right there, in the next room. He knew her name. He called even *Buddy* by his name.

Steffi clenched her teeth. She wasn't as important as a dog. She stood up and took her dishes to the sink. She turned on the water and poured in detergent, ignoring the thumping that had grown louder than before.

"Gol dang it! I know you're out there!" Vic shouted.

Steffi spun around and went into his room. Her frustration and anger came boiling up from deep inside. "If you know I'm here, and you want me, why can't you call my name?" she demanded.

The old man stared into her face. "You're just like *him*," he said.

"Who? Like my dad? I'd be proud to be like him. He was a good man. He worked hard, doing something he loved, and he took care of us the best he knew how. He was fun to be with, and he never yelled at me, and he said thanks when I did something for him, and he wasn't a . . . a *hypocrite!*" She practically spat the last word at him, unable to hold back the furious tears.

Vic still looked ferocious but surprised, too. "What's that supposed to mean?"

He still clutched the crutch he'd been pounding with, and she began to wonder if he were going to hit her with it, but she didn't back up.

Mom had told her that sometimes she didn't know enough to shut up, and maybe this was one of those times. Mom had also cautioned her against talking back to adults, but Steffi felt swept along as if she were caught in a strong current that wouldn't let her stop.

"Well?" Vic said through gritted teeth.

"It means you are a nasty, ungrateful, bad-tempered old man," Steffi said, not bothering to wipe away the dampness on her cheeks, "who says grace and reads the Bible and doesn't believe a word of it!"

Vic's wrath seemed tempered with shock. "What you saying, girl? How dare you talk to me like that?"

"Because it's true," Steffi said, though some of her own anger was fading in sheer grief and exhaustion. "You act like you believe in God, but you can't forgive anybody. You can't forgive my dad for doing what was right for *him* and you hate me because my mom sent me here without knowing for sure you got her letter or that it was okay—and she was wrong, she shouldn't have done it, but it's not *my* fault! I've tried to help, ever since I got here, and especially since you got hurt. I never ran even a house before, let alone a whole campground, and I'm doing the best I can! And I don't believe my grand-mother would have allowed you to be such a sour, dis-agreeable old man!"

Vic froze. He was still holding the crutch and his knuckles went white from gripping it so hard.

For the space of seconds they glared at each other, both of them breathing hard.

Steffi regained partial composure first, though the tears continued to stream down her face as she groped in her pocket for a tissue. "What did you want?"

"I wanted you to take the tray away," Vic said harshly.

"You already put it on the nightstand, so what was the hurry?" Steffi demanded with a stubbornness she hadn't known she possessed. "You knew I was eating my own supper. I'd have come in for your tray in a few more minutes. Did you treat my grandmother this way? I'm surprised she stayed with you after my dad left, and I don't blame him for going. He always told me if you couldn't say something good about somebody, to keep still. No wonder he never talked about you."

Vic forgot to breathe for a few heartbeats. Then some of the fury began to fade from his weathered counte-nance. He looked very strange, but Steffi couldn't inter-pret his expression.

It would have been nice if he'd apologized, but he didn't. After a moment more of silence, Steffi swal-lowed, blew her nose, and picked up the tray and carried it out to the kitchen.

She put the scraps and two chop bones in Buddy's bowl, washed the dishes and left them to drain, and still there was only silence from the bedroom.

"Fine," Steffi muttered under her breath, so that

Buddy stopped chewing and looked at her. "Let him rot, then. Unless he can call me by name, let him wait on himself."

The sound of an incoming vehicle gave her a welcome excuse to flee, leaving Buddy gnawing on a bone behind her.

13

The newcomers were a couple in their thirties, attractive, casually dressed. They had a pickup and were pulling one of those bullet-shaped silvery trailers.

"Got a space for tonight?" the man called out as Steffi emerged onto the porch.

"One night? Yes, if you can get by without a sewer connection. It's the only space we have left. There is a dump, over there."

"Sounds okay," the man said. "We'll come in and register."

There was something about the Nelsons that was different, though Steffi wasn't sure what it was. The woman looked around in the store, picking up a few odds and ends while the man signed up. She asked about laundry facilities, and went back to check them out.

After a moment Steffi realized that they both seemed to be looking the place over very carefully. Almost as if they wanted to be sure of the layout of the entire camp. Almost as if they were casing the joint.

Which was absurd, of course. Why would anyone with larcenous intentions come to a little park like this one? Nobody would expect to find anything worth stealing here, would they?

They smiled, and paid, and were quite pleasant. "Any pets?" Steffi asked. "They have to be leashed, and cleaned up after."

"No pets," they both said.

It was only after they'd left to park their rig that Steffi realized they hadn't taken their receipt and the tag to place in their front window. Not that anybody had trouble keeping track of who was there legitimately, with so few overnighters, but Vic always gave them the tag with the space number on it, so Steffi had been doing it, too.

Well, she supposed she'd better take it to them. No sense giving Vic anything else to be annoyed about. Besides, she didn't want to go back to the living quarters. She wasn't up to confronting Vic again yet.

It was hard to believe she'd actually said the things she had to her grandfather. Not that she didn't mean them— he *was* a nasty, bad-tempered old man—but it surprised her that she'd had the nerve to give voice to her thoughts.

Kurt Vail was still sitting beside his camper, watching the newcomers maneuver into their space. He lifted a hand in greeting to Steffi, though he didn't smile or try to talk to her the way he usually did.

The Nelsons got out of the truck and were standing beside it, talking, when she walked over to them.

"You need this to put in your window," she said, extending the tag. "And you forgot your receipt."

Mrs. Nelson smiled and accepted them both. "Thank you."

Mr. Nelson wasn't doing anything about hooking up to the electricity or the water. He was looking back toward the lake.

Inside their trailer, something clattered.

Steffi was already turning away, but she hesitated. They had said there were only two in their party, and that they had no pets. So who was making noises in the trailer?

She knew people sometimes tried to cheat, not wanting to pay for extra guests, but in a campground as small as this one they could hardly expect to get away with that. Was it worth challenging them for the few dollars' difference it would make?

She must have looked funny, because they were both suddenly aware. "Umm," Mrs. Nelson said. "We must have jiggled something loose on the way in here. I hope we didn't break anything."

They'd been parked for five minutes. Why would anything that came loose have waited this long to fall?

Uncertainly, Steffi continued to hesitate. She noticed Mrs. Nelson's left hand. She wasn't wearing a wedding ring.

Casually, Mrs. Nelson stuck that hand into a pocket. She smiled again, and turned away. "I'll check it out," she said.

Not all married women wore wedding rings, of course. And not all couples who traveled together were necessarily married to each other.

She decided to heck with it. The campground wasn't hers, and she didn't want the responsibility of enforcing all the rules on Vic's behalf.

The front porch only had a little sand on it. It didn't really need sweeping. But Steffi got out the broom; anything was better than going back in where Vic was. For all she knew, he might throw her out, right now. Then what would she do?

Helen would take her in. Steffi might have to share the couch with Barkley, but she wouldn't spend the night in the open.

A blue pickup jounced up to the foot of the steps, and Chester Taylor got out. He looked as sloppy as ever. "Need some smokes," he told Steffi.

She stepped inside and set the broom in the corner, to finish the job later. Chester followed her into the store and dug out his wallet while she got the cigarettes. He already reeked of tobacco and sweat, and she stepped back away from him. He hadn't brushed his teeth lately, either.

"Pa—"

Chester turned to where his son had just come in. "You got supper ready?"

"No," Burt said. "I gotta talk to you—"

"It wouldn't hurt you to fix something to eat if I ain't there when you get home ahead of me. You knew I was going to the city today, that I'd be late."

"Pa, it's important."

Chester scowled and walked toward his son. Steffi

wondered if he were going to hit him again, right here in front of a witness.

Burt said something in a low voice. Chester stopped stuffing his wallet back into a hip pocket. "You sure?"

"Yeah. You want I should pack a few things—"

"No. Leave 'em." He looked back at Steffi, and for some reason she felt a chill run through her. But it was Burt he spoke to, without looking at him as he finished dealing with his wallet. "You do something stupid?"

"Me? No. No, I didn't do anything."

"What brought him here, then?" Chester's expression suddenly showed realization and anger. "You get into that money? You spend any of it?"

Burt's mouth opened and closed without any words.

Without warning Chester swung one meaty arm, his open palm connecting with his son's face, knocking the boy sideways. "You did, didn't you? You spent some of that money, and you brought the feds down on us! You idiot! You moron! I *told* you not to touch it!"

Burt lifted a hand to his bleeding lip. "It was only a few dollars—"

"All it took was one lousy bill with a serial number they could trace! Every bank in the country had a list of those numbers! I told you we had to wait until it worked out we could head for Canada without making anybody suspicious! Over a year we been waiting, and you *blew* it!"

Bank robbers? Casey had kidded about robbing a bank, but had the Taylors actually done it? Was that why the FBI agent had come here?

Steffi cringed at the stream of abuse and profanity that spewed from Chester's mouth.

"We got to get out of here," the man said finally. "Grab a few things to take with us. Stuff to eat, without cooking it. Get me three or four cartons of cigarettes, I can't stand them Canadian ones."

"He ain't gonna let us drive out of here!" Burt protested.

Chester's gaze was fixed on Steffi, behind the counter. "Yeah, he will," Chester said in a calmer voice. "Because we're gonna take Steffi here as a hostage. He won't take a chance on her getting shot."

Steffi felt as if she were going to black out. He couldn't be serious!

"Hurry up! Take some of them cupcake things, and something to drink, too."

Steffi was having trouble breathing, and her hands were like ice. She was pinned behind the counter, with nowhere to run. She'd seen hundreds of scenes like this in the movies, and often her father had filled in for the actor playing either the villain or the hero as they struggled over the rescue of the heroine.

Only this wasn't the movies, and there was no hero. What in heaven's name could she do?

"Stash it in the truck," Chester ordered as Burt crammed a final package of cookies into the bag he was holding. "And get the shotgun off the rack and have it in sight if that Vail tries to interfere. Then open the door on my side of the truck, and little Steffi and I will join you."

A wild bird was beating itself to death in Steffi's chest. She put a hand over it and forced herself to breathe.

"Okay. Come on, sissy, let's go," Chester said.

Steffi couldn't move. Her mouth was so dry she couldn't even speak.

"Come on," Chester repeated, looking ugly. "You won't get hurt if you do what you're told."

He took several quick steps and grabbed her roughly by the arm, dragging her out from behind the small counter.

She stumbled, but he jerked her to her feet, then swung her up against him, forcing her to move ahead of him toward the outer door.

The smell of him almost gagged her, or perhaps it was only her own fear. He wrapped a beefy arm around her throat and shoved her forward.

Afterward she couldn't have said whether her reaction as they reached the doorway was considered or instinctive.

Steffi struggled, helpless to prevent being shoved along ahead of the man. She reached out her hands on both sides to try to prevent being dragged out to Chester's truck. Her fingers encountered something that came free in her hands, and she pulled the broom handle across the opening.

14

They stopped so abruptly that the broom handle cut into Steffi's abdomen. Even Chester grunted as some of the air went out of him, too.

And then, as she sensed Chester's rage building to a maniacal level, there was a solid *thwap* behind her. Chester loosened his stranglehold on her throat, and the broom slid clattering across the porch. Steffi staggered after it.

Chester lurched toward her, sagging, and the *thwap* came again, sending him to his knees.

Steffi caught a full breath of welcome air and turned to see her grandfather poised with his crutch ready to strike again.

Chester rolled toward him, snarling, but to Steffi's vast relief, new players suddenly entered the game.

"Stay right where you are, Taylor," Kurt Vail said; in his voice there was a note of authority Steffi hadn't heard before. "Put your hands behind you. Cuff him, Koontz, and read him his rights."

Steffi was still trying to get enough air into her lungs to make them stop hurting. It was Mrs. Nelson—or Koontz, or whatever her name was—who stepped forward efficiently with handcuffs.

And Mr. Nelson—or whoever *he* was—bent over to help Koontz haul Chester to his feet. "You have the right to remain silent," he began.

Mr. Vail stood beside the pickup. "Put the shotgun back in the rack, Burt. You're surrounded by armed federal agents. You don't want anybody to get hurt. It could mean spending the rest of your life in jail."

Burt, white-faced, was already clipping the gun back into its rack. "I didn't rob that bank," he said. "Nor shoot that guard, either. It was him that did it."

"But you spent some of the money, didn't you?" Vail reached for Burt's arm to assist him out of the truck.

"Was that what did it? Somebody traced that money I spent?"

Vail didn't answer that. "Cuff him, too," he said to the female federal agent called Koontz.

Chester glared at them all, but especially at his son. "You stupid fool, I told you. I told you. When I get my hands on you—"

Agent Koontz nudged him. "That's enough. Move, back over this way. Watch your step."

Vic, still wielding the crutch, was tottering. Mr. Vail helped him toward the living quarters. "Let's get you sitting down, here, sir."

"I am a little shaky," Vic admitted, allowing himself to be steered toward the nearest straight chair.

"It wasn't supposed to go down this way, right in the middle of camp," Mr. Vail said. "We brought in four agents in the trailer, and there were others waiting for Taylor to come out of camp with the boy. On their way out, the Taylors would have been stopped. Only Steffi got in the way." He glanced toward her, where she stood just inside the living room.

"I thought he was going to kill me," Steffi said, rubbing her throat where it still hurt.

"We weren't going to let that happen. But that was a pretty good assist your grandpa gave us, whacking him over the head with the heavy end of his crutch. You and Steffi were quite a team, Vic, with a crutch and a broom handle."

Vic was visibly trembling from the exertion. "We were, weren't we?"

"I thought you were flat in bed," Steffi said, forgetting that they'd parted on less than amiable terms.

"I got heartburn," Vic stated. "Couldn't raise anybody by hollering, so I got up to go into the store and get some antacid tablets. When I overheard what was going on, I didn't know what to do. But I couldn't let that miserable lout kidnap my granddaughter, could I?"

He still hadn't called her by name, but he'd said, "my granddaughter." Steffi marveled at it.

"Look after each other," Mr. Vail said. "I have some business to finish."

He brushed past Casey to leave the room. Casey beamed enthusiastically. "Wow! This is just like being in the movies, isn't it?"

"Not quite," Steffi said. She had to sit down, too; her legs were shaking. "In the movies you know it's going to turn out okay. I wasn't sure about this. Chester was really strong for somebody who's supposed to be on a disability pension; I thought he was going to kill me with his bare hands."

"Probably the disability was a scam, too," Casey asserted. "Several times we saw him lifting things that seemed pretty heavy for a guy with a bad back. I suppose he needed the disability to live on until they could take the stolen money and run to Canada with it. Dad thinks there's a good chance he was responsible for some of the small thefts around town, too, though nobody ever caught him at anything." He turned to look at Vic. "You were great, Vic! You really swung that crutch!" Casey applauded.

"It was all I had," Vic said. "He was between me and the phone, and I didn't have the coins on me to use it anyway, so I couldn't call the police."

"The cops were already here. A whole bunch of them." Casey was eager to share his knowledge. "Some of them came into camp in that new trailer, and there were others staked out along the road; that's where they expected to arrest Chester, when he tried to leave camp. You know, I'll bet Agent Vail dropped his ID on purpose today, knowing someone would find it and spread the word. And it would spook Chester into running, just like it did."

"Why didn't he tell the rest of us?" Steffi asked. Immediately she knew the answer herself. "I guess FBI agents don't explain things to the neighbors, do they? I heard someone inside that new trailer, but I thought the

Nelsons—or whoever they are—were trying to smuggle in some relatives or something. Mr. Vail was here in camp a long time before they made their move."

"Burt swiped some of the money Chester had hidden away, and spent it in town," Casey was happy to explain. "A teller at the bank checked on the serial numbers and called it in, and they sent someone to investigate. Agent Vail was due to go on vacation anyway, so he came here and snooped around, trying to figure out where Chester hid the money he stole. When he had it located, he called in reinforcements and they scared Chester into trying to run. It wasn't supposed to endanger anyone."

Casey was obviously enjoying the entire episode, which annoyed her a little. She had believed she was going to be kidnapped and maybe killed. If it hadn't been for Vic swinging that crutch, the Taylors might have gotten away with it. She was pretty sure Chester had been right, that the federal agents wouldn't have fired on him while he'd been using Steffi as a shield.

"I suppose the usually close-mouthed FBI told you all this?" Steffi asked.

"Well, no," Casey admitted. "My dad listened to them talking and figured most of it out. And we saw part of it, of course. How'd you think to grab that broom, Steffi, and keep Chester from pushing you out onto the porch? You really threw him off balance."

She shrugged, not sure of the answer.

Buddy had finally forsaken his chop bones to investigate what was going on in the living room. He sidled up to Steffi and rested his big head on her knee. She began to scratch behind his ears. "Where did they hide the money they stole?"

"In town. Dad didn't hear them say exactly where it was hidden, but I think around that gas station where Burt works. Chester left his fingerprints on your arm, Steffi."

She inspected the purple marks. "Probably on my neck, too. And I'll bet that crutch made some marks on Chester." Suddenly she started to giggle, feeling a bit hysterical now that it was all over. She stopped when she saw Vic's face. He wasn't amused. In fact, he looked pretty stressed out.

"Thanks for rescuing me," she told her grandfather.

Did he nod a little bit, or did she imagine it?

"Boy," he said to Casey, "give me a hand, back to bed. I'm wore out."

"Sure," Casey said, and quickly crossed the room.

Steffi watched them go, feeling pretty well "wore out" herself. Buddy licked at her hand, and she fondled his ears. It seemed odd that she felt like crying, now that the danger was past, and she groped in a pocket for a tissue.

"Steffi, you all right?"

She quickly wiped her eyes and rose to meet her visitors, which seemed to include practically everybody in the campground. She assured them she was fine, except for a few bruises, and so was Vic.

"My, such excitement!" Elwood said, leading the gathering into the small living room. "I wonder if we'll all wind up on the evening news?"

"Not our pictures, certainly," Oliver told him. "There weren't any TV cameras around. Okay if we go see Vic for a minute, Steffi? We hear he really beat up on old Chester."

He didn't wait for permission, but went on through to Vic's bedroom, followed by Elwood.

Helen, holding Barkley in her arms, sank onto the sofa next to Steffi. "You were so brave, dear! I'd have been frightened out of my mind!"

"I was," Steffi admitted. The Montonis stood in the doorway, and Mr. Montoni waggled a hand at her. "Glad you're okay, Steffi. See you tomorrow."

Helen was gazing at her with something like awe. "I've been hiding for so long, and it's been such a strain. Do you think that Mr. Vail is right? I talked to him for a minute before they took the Taylors away. He says I'm as much in my right mind as anybody, and Eunice can't *make* me go into a rest home, or move away from here, where I can keep Barkley. I would die of loneliness without Barkley."

"I'm sure Mr. Vail knows," Steffi told her. "Eunice can talk a lot, but she can't force you to give up Barkley and go into a home."

Helen sighed and shook her head. "All this time, I thought she could do what she threatened to do. Well, let's go home, Barkley." She turned a sunny smile on Steffi and rose to her feet. "See you tomorrow, dear."

Casey came through from the kitchen as Helen left. He was grinning. "You'd think Vic was Superman, the way they're building him up. Actually, he *was* pretty good, wasn't he? The Taylors had guns, and all Vic had was a crutch."

"He was pretty good," Steffi agreed.

Later that night, when everyone had stopped talking about what had happened and gone home, long after the silvery trailer and Kurt Vail and the federal agents had gone away, Steffi stepped to the door of Vic's room.

"Do you want anything else before I go to bed?" she asked uncertainly.

"No," Vic said. And then, sounding rusty as if the effort of saying the words was almost more than he could manage, "No, thanks."

Near the pit of her stomach, Steffi felt a stirring of something warm. She hesitated, then said, "I found a list of Grandma's relatives in the Bible. Some of them are my cousins, I think. Do you know where they are?"

For a few seconds she thought he wouldn't answer. Then, still sounding like a squeaky gate, Vic said, "Some of 'em over to Cadillac. Rest around Petoskey."

"Umm. Thanks. Good night, then."

She was halfway to her own room when she heard his muttered, "'Night."

She was tired, but not sleepy. Once she'd gotten into bed and Buddy had climbed up to rest his head on her feet, she adjusted the little lamp and reached in the drawer beside her for a pencil and a pad of paper.

Dear Mom, she began to write. *It hasn't been nearly as boring here as I expected it to be. Vic didn't get your letter, so he wasn't too happy when I showed up. But everybody else here has been really nice, almost like a family. Except for the Taylors, but the FBI took them away, so they won't bother anybody anymore. We've got the swimming pool ready to use again, so that's a help, and we had a big picnic. I painted all the signs, and more customers are coming in. I can't tell if Vic likes that or not; he never says anything about them. Actually, he doesn't say much, period. He thinks Mexican food is exotic, and anything anybody eats or does in California is pretty far out.*

She hesitated, chewing on her eraser. *Maybe Vic is coming around a little, though. He rescued me from the kidnappers and bank robbers.*

In his sleep, Buddy breathed a deep sigh, and Steffi smiled and finished her letter. *I think tomorrow I'll try a tamale casserole and see if Vic will eat an extra helping of it. Love, Steffi.*

If the letter didn't induce her mom to call and get the details in person, now that she had the number for the pay phone, Steffi would be very, very surprised.